WOLF PRINCE

M GUIDA

1

Never in a billion years would I have thought I'd be heading toward a supernatural academy, riding a silver dragon to meet with an ancient vampire. The last vampire I encountered tried to kill me, and I wasn't sure how I felt about meeting one that was a thousand times more powerful.

I glanced over my right shoulder and smiled at Hades, the little Catalan dragon with the head of a lion and a body covered in scales. He had no problem keeping up with Raven. Over these past few weeks, he'd become my buddy. I knew I couldn't have gotten through this turmoil without him.

I clutched Raven's neck tightly. Besides being a dragon, she had two other bloodlines—vampire and Golden Demon—which made her the most powerful being in our world. I doubt even King Calvin would take her on, but this wasn't her fight. It was mine.

As she flew over pine and aspen treetops, the moonlight glistened on the snow covering their branches. A cold wind blew through my hair and froze my bones. My teeth wouldn't stop chattering. Poor Ashton. Raven was clutching him in her talons, and he must have been a frozen popsicle by now. He was already in pretty bad shape from the torture inflicted on him at Iredale

Palace after, my uncle, King Calvin, had discovered that he was a traitor. But Raven said there was a Fae doctor at Legacy Academy who could heal him. I hoped she was right.

Through the trees, I saw turrets with flags flapping in the wind and Raven started to descend. That had to be Legacy Academy. It was a huge castle that reminded me of Sleeping Beauty's castle at Disneyland, but much bigger. Uneasiness pooled and settled in my gut as I thought of meeting the ancient vampire. I held onto Raven's neck tightly as she aimed for the snow-covered courtyard.

A tall man was waiting for us in the courtyard and my stomach clenched. Oh, God. That had to be him.

Stay Calm Stay Calm Stay Calm

Raven gently released Ashton onto the snow and I slid off her back. I immediately knelt down next to Ashton who was still unconscious. He was deathly white and barely breathing.

Hades landed next to Ashton and sniffed. He looked up at me with sorrowful eyes and whined.

I pushed Ashton's thick blond hair out of his eyes. "Can you hear me?"

All I got was a weak groan.

Someone knelt next to me. "I'll send for Dr. Greenwood."

I slowly lifted my head to stare into the almost-black eyes of my host. The wind blew his long dark brown hair behind him and his thick robe hugged his broad shoulders.

He smiled. "Hello, Salem. It's nice to finally meet you. I'm Anton Lange, the Headmaster of Legacy Academy. Welcome to my home."

"Can you help Ashton?" I asked him worriedly.

"Of course, my child. We have a wonderful Fae healer at Legacy." He scooped Ashton's limp body into arms. "Follow me, please."

Anton climbed a flight of stairs and then led me into one of the brick buildings. Hades was right behind me. I wasn't sure where Raven had gone. I was too preoccupied with Ashton.

Anton kicked open the door. "Dr. Greenwood? I have a patient for you."

I blinked, not believing what I was seeing. It looked more like a spa than a medical ward. Rather than smelling of antiseptic, the fragrance of eucalyptus and some other healing herbs filled my nostrils, making me want to have a massage. Comforters in a daisy print covered twin beds, and there were even daisies in vases on the nightstands next to the beds. Honestly, if more hospital rooms looked like this, maybe patients wouldn't mind going there.

Another tall, elegant man came out of a back room, yawning. He had long blond hair and was wearing a robe that sparkled as he moved. Concern filled his blues eyes that were flecked with brown and green. "Headmaster, what's wrong?"

Anton lowered Ashton gently onto a bed. "It's Ashton Shaw. Looks like he's been hurt pretty badly."

Dr. Greenwood hurried over and put his palm on Ashton's forehead. Then he frowned. "He's in a great amount of pain. His wolf is trying to shield his human side from it."

I bit my lip and shoved a hand through my tangled hair. "Can you help him?"

Anton tilted his head. "Dr. Greenwood, this is Salem Willis, the missing Wolf Princess."

Dr. Greenwood flashed his gaze over me. "So you're the one that Mateo sent word about. It is wonderful to meet you, but for now you must excuse me. I must attend to Ashton."

I dropped my arm. "Of course. Please do." I slowly sat in a chair near Ashton's bed, preparing to keep watch over him.

"Dr. Greenwood will take care of Ashton, Salem. You look exhausted and need some rest."

I shook my head, still not quite sure if I should trust him. I couldn't shake the memory of the other vampire who had attacked me at my aunt's house. "No. I think I should stay with him."

"Your aunt is also a guest in my home. Will you not follow me? I can take you to her."

I hesitated, not sure what to do. Hades rubbed my leg as if to say it was all right. I was so glad he was here.

Dr. Greenwood looked at me. "There's nothing you can do right now, Salem. Get some rest and then you can see Ashton tomorrow."

"I promise you, Ashton is in excellent hands," Anton said. "Shall we go?"

"Can Hades come?" I blurted.

He laughed. "I think I would have a hard time peeling him away from you." He opened the door. "Please, this way."

Weariness came over me. I glanced down at Ashton and kissed him softly on the lips. "I'll be back tomorrow, my prince."

Ashton's lips didn't move.

I fought back tears as I held his limp hand. "What if I leave and something happens to him overnight?"

Dr. Greenwood put his hand on my shoulder. "Ashton will not die, Salem. He's come to the right place. I promise you he'll be awake tomorrow, but he needs rest—as do you."

I sighed heavily, knowing there wasn't anything else I could do. I headed toward the door with Hades at my side, then glanced over my shoulder one last time to look at Ashton. He was lying so still on that bed and his face was paler than the pillowcase.

Please, please, please, let him be okay

Tonight, between Ashton being wounded and Mateo being forced to play spy, I knew I would have a hard time sleeping. Either one of them could come to an untimely death because of me.

"Come, Salem," Anton urged.

I reluctantly followed him out of the infirmary, praying Ashton would be awake tomorrow. In my experience, doctors weren't always exactly trustworthy. I hoped Dr. Greenwood would prove me wrong.

"Is my aunt awake?" I asked as he led me to a tower.

"She's been unable to sleep a wink worrying about you."

The tower door whipped open and my Aunt Remi raced over to me, pressing her palms against my cheeks. "Thank God you're okay."

I hugged her. "I'm so glad you're alive."

"Velkan and his demon wolves attacked. Hades and I didn't have time to grab the Rose Box." She burst into tears. "I'm so sorry."

"Don't worry." I kissed her cheek. "We'll get it back."

She sniffed. "I hope so. Anton tells me that's the key to your regaining your crown."

I yawned. "That's what Raven told me, too." I scanned the courtyard. "Where is Raven, anyway?"

"She's inside with her mate, Lucien," said Anton. "He's been worried about her."

Remi chuckled. "I don't think we'll see either one of them until morning."

Heat warmed my cheeks as I thought of what they were probably doing. "So...now what?"

"I suggest you get some much-needed rest," Anton said.

I frowned. "Won't Calvin know I'm here?"

Anton shrugged. "Probably, but it will take him some time to get here, and by then you'll be gone." He stuck out his arm. "Follow me, Salem. I have a bed prepared for you."

Hades growled.

Anton laughed. "Don't worry, buddy. You'll be sleeping in the same room."

Hades nudged my leg as if to say 'don't worry, I'm not leaving you.'

Anton escorted us through his quarters. They looked like Dracula had been his interior decorator. Long red velvet drapes covered the windows and the French doors that I suspected went out on a patio. The leather loveseat and couch were the same deep crimson and went perfectly with the hand-carved mahogany coffee table and end tables. A fire flickered in the white marble fireplace, chasing away the chill.

It was all so inviting that I wanted to grab one of his thick afghans and curl up on the leather couch with Hades at my feet.

Then my eye was caught by the sword with glittering moonstones in the handle lying on a nightstand next to my bed.

"My sword!" I thought I had lost it. I ran over and picked it up. The familiar sensations ran up and down my arm and I felt like I was one with it once again. I grinned wildly. "Where did you find this? I thought Calvin had taken it."

"Mateo. He was able to retrieve it from the stolen artifacts room and give it to Raven."

My smile died on my face. "Won't Calvin find out it's missing?"

"Perhaps. But Mateo thought it was worth the risk."

My stomach clenched, not sure I agreed. I glanced up at Anton. "Is the witch's *Book of Goody* here?"

"Yes. It's in my study."

Renewed eagerness swelled inside me. "May I please look at it?"

"In time. You need sleep, Salem. It is a powerful spell book and you must be well rested before you even attempt to look at it. If you're in a weakened state, spells can go very badly." His warning stomped all over my eagerness and my weariness came back with a vengeance.

The last thing I wanted was for a spell to go wrong. There was too much at stake.

And he was right: I was dead tired, tired of fighting demon wolves, tired of staying one step ahead of my crafty uncle. Tired of it all.

Remi rubbed my back. "Salem, you look like you're going to fall asleep on your feet. You need to get to bed. Come on, Hades." She linked her arm through mine. "This way, darlin'. Good night, Anton."

"Good night," he said. "Salem, you and Ashton are safe. Legacy's walls will keep you out of harm's way."

Remi led me down a hallway and then opened a door that led to a beautiful Dracula-style bedroom with a red canopy bed. I could hardly wait to stretch out on it. There was even a marble fireplace.

"Anton sure does like nice things."

"He's an ancient vampire," Remi said. "He has loads of money, and his heart rests here at the Academy. He'd do anything to keep it looking good—and to protect it."

I sat on the bed. "Am I putting him and everybody else here in danger?"

Hades hopped up on the bed and laid his head on my thigh. I stroked his mane gently, glad he was going to be guarding me tonight.

Remi stacked some logs in the fireplace. "This isn't the first time that enemies have tried to penetrate these walls and I suspect it won't be the last. But with Raven, her mate Lucien and Anton all here, I don't think Calvin will attack just yet." She crumpled up some paper and placed it under the grate. "He'll wait until you're the most vulnerable."

Shivering, I rubbed my arms. "You mean after I leave here?"

Remi lit a match on the stone hearth and the kindling ignited, stirring up a blazing flame. She lowered her head. "I'm sorry to say it, but yes."

"This is all a little overwhelming. What if Mateo gets caught spying?"

She sat next to me on the bed and I laid my head on her shoulder. "Salem, he knows the risk he's taking, but he thinks it's worth it. Calvin is a cruel king. The people deserve to have the rightful heir sitting on the throne."

The fear and sorrow building up inside me burst forth and swirled around like an angry winter storm. I grabbed her shirt and buried my tearful face in her shoulder. "But what if...what if

Calvin tortures Mateo like he did Ashton? People..." I bit back a sob. "People are getting hurt because of me."

Remi wrapped her arms around me, hugging me close. "Salem, what Calvin did to your parents and what he's continuing to do to his people is terribly wrong. His evil knows no bounds. You have to stop him."

I looked up at her through blurry eyes. "What if I can't?"

She kissed my forehead. "I know you can, Salem. You have the first king's blood running through your veins. That's why Calvin is so afraid of you and is determined to kill you."

I took a deep, quaking breath. "The war is going to get worse, isn't it?"

She rubbed my back. "I'm afraid so. The storm is coming, Salem. You can't stop it, but you're not alone in this war. You have friends. That's something that Calvin doesn't have, for all his power."

I pulled away and wiped the tears off my face. "What do you mean? He has loads of alliances."

She cupped my chin in her hands and looked tenderly into my eyes. "That doesn't mean they are his friends. They could turn on him on a dime. Calvin doesn't understand love and friendship. That will be his undoing."

I thought of how he treated his daughter, Gloria, and hoped Remi was right. I knew I had friends that would back me up, but in the end, it would be me squaring off with Calvin alone.

He wasn't the only one who was afraid. Facing him scared the wolf out of me.

2

The next day, I woke with Hades sleeping at my feet. The fire in the hearth was still roaring and I wondered if magic had kept the flames going all night. I stretched out luxuriously like a cat, arching my back. A warm blue sweater, underwear, lacy bra, and a pair of leggings were all draped over a nearby chair. Next to my sword was a belt with a sheath. I hoped either Remi or Raven had left everything there and not Anton. It felt creepy for a male vampire to be picking out my undergarments.

But then again, beggars couldn't be choosers and I hadn't brought a suitcase. There wasn't an alarm clock next to the bed but I didn't need it. My stomach told me it was time to get up.

I stroked Hades' soft body. "I'm going to take a shower, buddy."

He yawned and buried himself deeper into the covers.

I grabbed my new clothes and hurried into a bathroom that blew my mind. Man, did Anton love luxury. I had never been in a white and black marble bathroom, let alone with golden fixtures. I felt like I had stepped into a billionaire's home.

Then again, according to my aunt, maybe I had. She'd said Anton had money, lots of it.

I turned on the shower but instead of water coming out of a single shower head it was like a rainstorm dropping from the ceiling. This was so out of my league.

I stripped out of the nightshirt I had found in one of the dresser drawers last night and hopped into my dream shower. Hot water softly splattered and massaged my aching muscles. I could stand in here all day, twirling around under this glorious waterfall. It was Heaven.

It wasn't every day I got to enjoy the most luxurious shower ever so I stayed where I was until finally, an hour later, the water ran cold. I stepped out and quickly got dressed and sheathed my sword in my belt. I wasn't going anywhere without it again.

When I opened the door, Hades stretched himself awake on the bed and yawned.

I laughed. "Have you been sleeping this whole time, lazy bones?"

His tail twitched as he glided off the bed, opening his wings. He landed at my feet and then shook his body as he closed his wings again.

"Come on, boy. I bet you're hungry."

Hades immediately headed toward the door and I opened it to a smell of frying bacon and the wonderful smell of fresh roasted coffee. My stomach let out a loud roar.

The little Catalan dragon looked up at me as if he were grinning.

"Guess I'm hungry too, dude. Let's see what's cooking."

Remi greeted me in the hallway. "I was just coming to get you two. Anton has a breakfast fit for a queen all ready."

"Sounds good to me." I hoped he wasn't doing this on my account—gosh, what was I thinking. Not me, Raven. She was destined to be the next queen of the Golden Demons.

Hades and I followed Remi to the dining room and my mouth immediately watered. The table was laden with platters filled with gooey cinnamon rolls, plump sausages, crispy bacon, and scrambled eggs.

"Would you like some coffee?" Remi asked as she headed over to a sideboard with a silver urn and a matching silver cream jug and sugar bowl.

"Absolutely. Lots of cream, please, if you don't mind."

"No trouble."

Raven walked in, looking refreshed. Her dark hair was pulled up into a loose bun and she had on a Legacy sweatshirt and jeans. She was so petite that it always blew my mind to think that she was the most powerful supernatural in our world.

A tall, muscular guy with long curly hair and dark eyes was right at her side, walking with a swagger that said he was used to getting his way.

"Good morning, Salem. I was wondering when you were going to get up." She clutched the guy's thick bicep and looked up at him with an adoring gaze. "This is my mate, Lucien Acosta."

He pulled a chair out for Raven as he smiled. "Nice to finally meet you, Salem."

I frowned. "You've heard of me?"

"Please. *Everyone's* heard of you." He grinned again, a grin that reached the corners of his eyes, making him even look more handsome. "You're the missing wolf princess."

Anton came in with a plate of hash browns that he set down on the table. "Good morning. I hope everyone's hungry."

Hunger flared in Raven's eyes. "Absolutely. Everything looks and smells delicious."

Anton picked up a dish and immediately filled it with eggs, bacon, and sausage. "Here you go, Hades."

The little Catalan dragon raced over to his bowl and began to devour his breakfast happily as the rest of us sipped our coffee.

"Cinnamon roll?" Lucien passed the platter around.

Raven grinned. "No one would ever suspect it, but Anton's a great baker."

Anton lifted up a roll and examined it proudly. "One of my many talents, if I do say so myself."

I glanced around the table and frowned. There was water, and orange juice, but I couldn't see a pitcher or a glass filled with blood anywhere. I leaned close to Remi and lowered my voice to a whisper. "I don't get it. Don't vampires have to drink blood?"

Anton turned his gaze toward me as if he had overheard my question. "I'm an ancient vampire, Salem. I don't have to feed on blood every day. And when I do, it comes from blood banks." He cocked an eyebrow. "I don't feed on humans." He grinned wickedly as he picked up a piece of bacon. "Unless it's a willing human donor."

I frowned as I thought of my attacker who had wanted to rip out my throat.

Remi slipped a sly glance at me, smiling. "He means willing females who enjoy his... attentions."

"Oh," I said as I licked the sticky icing off my fingers. With his looks, I was sure he had no trouble getting women into his bed. I just hoped he really did leave them alive.

Remi dished up my plate with bacon, sausage, and eggs.

I gave her a big smile. "Thank you." She was always taking such good care of me—something I had never known growing up in foster care.

She winked and filled up her plate. I swear there was enough food to feed a small army.

Lucien polished off his last sausage. "So, Anton, have you given Salem the *Book of Goody* yet?"

"Not yet."

Raven frowned. "Why not?"

Anton got up and refilled his coffee cup. "Last night she was too tired. The book's powerful and can't be touched or used in a weakened state. It's too dangerous."

Remi's eyes darkened. "Maybe she shouldn't have it at all. She's a wolf—not a witch."

My gut tightened. So, we were back to pretending that we weren't witches, were we? Great.

"Remi." Anton flashed her a serious look. "Denying what you and Salem are will not change anything. I know you're frightened, but you're at Legacy Academy. Mixed blood is the norm here—not unusual at all."

She sighed. "I know, but openly admitting it...it could be dangerous."

Raven gave me an understanding look. "No more dangerous than it has been for Ebony and I." Bitterness seeped into her dark eyes and she poked the last bit of scrambled eggs around her plate with her fork. "My sister hasn't exactly gotten a warm reception from the Dark Demons, or the other royal kingdoms."

Lucien rubbed her back. "They'll come around soon, don't worry."

"Maybe. Maybe not. Only your dad has truly accepted her."

Lucien pushed away his plate. "Well, they're not exactly rolling out the royal carpet for Gunnar, either."

I looked at each of them. "From what I've seen so far, this world seems pretty set in its ways."

Anton put down his coffee cup. "No more so than the human one. As I recall, back in the 1960's it was unthinkable to have African Americans attend an all-White school. Things have changed since that time. They will change in our world, too." He smiled. "Raven and Ebony have already set things in motion." He winked at me. "And now, Salem, it's your turn to change history."

I didn't answer him. Changing history wasn't what I had in mind. Not getting killed and not letting anyone else I love get hurt were on my agenda instead.

I cleared my throat nervously. "So, based on what you said, this *Book of Goody* is filled with dark magic?"

Anton shook his head. "Not dark magic—just powerful."

I pushed my plate away that still had half a cinnamon roll and some eggs. This talk had made my stomach do funny flips and I'd lost my appetite. "Hayley said the *Book of Goody* would help me get in touch with my powers and learn how to control them. Do you think that's true?"

He nodded. "I do, but you must start slowly. If you try to use all the spells at once, it could overwhelm you."

"I'll keep that in mind."

He gave me a stern look. "Make sure you do. If you don't, the magic could kill you."

My eyes widened and my mouth dropped open as a tremor of fear ran through me, turning me into a quivering bowl of jelly.

Remi narrowed her eyes and clutched my shaking hand. "How is she supposed to master this book without getting herself killed, then?"

Anton didn't seem to be one bit fazed by Remi's growing anger. "By learning one spell at a time, starting with the very first. The spells will become more advanced as she moves on. Once she gets to a certain place, she'll realize that she has the strength to master the rest of the spells."

I found my voice. "Which will be when? I mean, how will I know that I'm strong enough?"

His eyes sparkled and he grinned. "You'll just know. I can't tell you how many spells you would need to have done to attain this level. It could be anywhere from one to a hundred or even a thousand."

I slid my fingers through my hair. "A thousand spells?"

"It's a very thick book," he said. "I suspect you will reach this master level when your wolf and your witch have become one."

"Clear as mud, as always," Lucien grumbled. "Some things never change."

I glanced over at Lucien who smiled at me. "Anton likes to speak in riddles."

Anton sat straighter in his chair. "Really? I thought I was being very clear."

Wow. If he thought that was being clear, I would hate to hear his idea of being vague. Already I felt like I was in way over my head.

"Salem," he said. "You'll find to accomplish this, you'll need the help of friends. You can't do this alone."

Uneasiness played havoc with my gut. "But I don't want any more people to get hurt like Ashton was."

He traced on the table with his finger as if trying to make a point. "A righteous path is rarely a straight line, or without obstacles. You must trust your friends as much as they do you."

Easier said than done.

"Speaking of my friends," I said timidly. "Would you mind if I checked on Ashton before I looked at that book?"

"Be my guest," he said. "This afternoon, we'll go over the book and then we'll come up with a plan for the next steps of your journey." He made it sound like I was going on a treasure hunt, not taking on my uncle, mastering the magical part of myself, and facing demon wolves. That didn't sound like an exciting journey to me, more of a cursed path.

I excused myself from the table and hurried over to the infirmary with Hades right on my heels. When I opened the door, I didn't see Dr. Greenwood anywhere and slid quietly into the empty chair next to Ashton's bed.

Hades plopped down at my feet. I was so glad he was with me. Nothing could have prepared me for what was in store here. Powerful magic books that could kill me if I wasn't very, very careful? It was all pretty overwhelming.

Ashton moaned, as if having a bad dream.

I squeezed his hand. "It's okay, Ashton. You're safe. You're at Legacy." My voice cracked and I could barely get the words out.

A lump of guilt swelled in my throat. He'd been tortured because of me. I held his limp hand, brushing my thumb over his flesh, wishing I could heal him.

Damn Calvin.

The door opened. Raven walked in, pulled over a chair, and sat next to me. "How is he?"

I breathed deeply, afraid I'd start blubbering. "He still hasn't woken up. I'm worried. What if he doesn't?" My voice trembled as I thought of losing him.

Raven clasped my arm. "Don't worry. Dr. Greenwood is a powerful Fae and his potions and spells have helped heal many of us."

I gave her a small smile but didn't answer.

She gave me a sympathetic look. "Salem, listen to me. What happened to Ashton isn't your fault."

"Yes, it is. He was tortured because of me."

"Salem. Calvin is evil. He is no different than Cormac and Ryker. He's hungry for power and determined to keep his crown, meanwhile you're the lost princess and supposed to retake the throne. Freedom is never free."

I blinked away the hated tears. "But more people could get hurt. Look what happened to Ashton. Velkan and the demon wolves almost captured Remi and Hades. And now Mateo's trapped back there. If he's discovered..." I couldn't finish.

She gently squeezed my arm again. "I know. But Ashton and Mateo are both willing to take the chance. And it's not just Ashton and Mateo that are suffering. Your people are too. You must take your rightful place. Calvin is an evil king."

I knew she was right, but it felt like she was piling more and more weight onto my already weary shoulders.

"Here. I brought you something." She handed me a clear crystal stone that was about the size of a paperweight.

I frowned. "What is this?"

"It's a magic orb. Anton gave it to me when I was studying here, desperate to rescue my mother." She laughed. "Well, maybe I should say I *took* the orb...and he allowed me to keep it. Now, I'm passing it on to you."

I looked at the orb curiously. "What does it do?"

She put her hand over mine. "It will show what you want most. Trust in it. It may not show you everything, but it will show you what you need most."

"Are you sure you want to give it to me?"

She nodded as she stood. "Absolutely. I must speak with Anton. I'll be back later to check on you and Ashton."

I frowned. "Speak with Anton? What about?"

"Ebony. I'm very worried about her. The Dark Demons are really giving her a rough time."

I tilted my head. "Then you should go."

She flashed me a warm smile. "Yes. I'll be back soon. I promise."

I clutched the orb and was surprised at how heavy it was. "Thank you."

"You're welcome." She glanced at Ashton and then back to me. "You remind me of me when I was here. You're faced with similar choices to those I had to make."

"You mean fighting Cormac and Ryker?"

"Actually, that was the easy part. The hard part was choosing between Bo and Lucien."

I frowned. "Bo? I haven't heard of him."

She blinked away tears and then cleared her throat. "Bo was the first guy at Legacy that tugged at my heart. I cared about both him and Lucien."

"What happened?"

"Bo was trying to protect me in one of our battles against Ryker."

"And?"

She bit her lip and her voice wobbled. "He didn't make it."

I gave her a hug. "I'm so sorry."

"Thank you."

We just held each other for a long moment, thinking of the men in our lives willing to die to protect us.

She untangled herself from our embrace. "I'd better go." She sighed heavily as she stared down at Ashton. "Just know I've been in your shoes, especially where love is concerned."

I gave her a you've-got-to-be-kidding-me look. "Believe me, finding love is the last thing on my mind."

Raven winked. "You're not fooling me, wolf girl." She gestured toward the orb. "Check it out and then we'll talk later."

She left the infirmary with me staring at the orb curiously, not sure how to use it.

Suddenly, clouds moved within the orb and I almost dropped it when the clouds started to take shape.

I gasped and clapped my hand over my mouth. "Mateo."

He was in some seriously deep shit.

3

*E*verything stopped in the infirmary—Hades' heavy breathing as he slept at my feet, Ashton's soft snores in his bed, the thundering of my heart. I sat frozen in my chair. My hand shook uncontrollably as I stared at the orb.

I couldn't breathe.

I couldn't move.

In the orb, I saw Mateo in a dimly-lit passageway. It was so narrow that I wasn't sure where in Iredale Palace this corridor was, if it was even there at all. It could be anywhere.

Flickering torches highlighted his handsome face and I saw with a pang that beads of sweat were breaking out across his forehead. He was backed up against a brick wall, as if he was cornered. Uneasiness flickered in his dark brown eyes as he kept scanning the passageway frantically.

Something was there.

Something was coming closer.

Something evil.

Dark shadows moved toward him. He braced his feet shoulder width apart and drew his sword. Bits of his long brown hair fell out of his man bun and stuck to his rugged cheeks.

The mysterious clouds took shape and my heart clenched at what I saw. The demon Velkan and his wolves were spread out around Mateo, cutting off any escape.

Velkan's red eyes glowed as he flashed Mateo an evil grin. "I knew I couldn't trust you."

Mateo met his gaze without a single ounce of fear. "I am captain of the Royal Guard. I would never do anything to hurt my king." His level voice didn't shake.

The flickering torches highlighted Velkan's long dark hair and made his shadow grow longer as it completely shrouded Mateo. "Yes, that's what you keep saying. But if that is true, then why were you trying to take the Rose Box?"

That's when I noticed that Velkan held the wooden box in his hands. Oh, God. What foolish thing had Mateo been trying to do?

Mateo shrugged. "I was merely going to move it to a more secure location. Then you and your demon wolves attacked me."

"You're a liar." Velkan laughed. "I think the good king should know what his Captain of the Guard has been up to. I'm sure he'd want to have a private conversation with you."

The glint in his eyes made me sit straighter in my chair.

Crapcrapcrapcrap

Calvin was going to torture him just like they had Ashton. And I was stuck here, not able to help him.

Shit.

Then the mysterious clouds rolled back over the orb like an angry thunderstorm, blocking Mateo and Velkan from view.

I shook it hard, trying to disperse the clouds, but they only darkened. "Dammit, you stupid orb. Show me Mateo. Show me what's happening." The words came out louder than I intended, shattering the silence in the infirmary.

Hades jerked up to all fours and growled menacingly as he scanned the room, hunting for an enemy.

"Salem, are you all right?" a calm voice asked behind me.

Tears blurred my vision as I twisted around in my chair. Anton headed over to me. I hadn't even heard him come into the room.

Dr. Greenwood rushed out of a back room. "What's going on out here?" His voice was less than pleased, but I didn't care.

I couldn't answer him. Someone else was going to get hurt again, or maybe even killed, because of me.

Dr. Greenwood hurried over to Ashton and put his palm on his forehead. "Headmaster, if she can't control herself, Salem will have to leave. My patient is in a deep healing sleep" ...he gave me a warning glare... "and cannot be wakened for any reason."

Anton sat on the twin bed next to Ashton's. "She won't wake your patient, Dr. Greenwood."

Dr. Greenwood gave me another disgruntled look and disappeared into the back room again.

Anton's dark eyes softened. "Now, Salem, tell me what happened."

I opened my shaking palm that revealed the orb. "Raven...Raven..."

I couldn't finish. My mind tossed around horrible images of what was probably happening to Mateo right this very minute as I sat on my ass doing nothing.

"Ah. I see Raven has given you the magic orb."

I bit my lip and nodded miserably.

Anton gave me a small smile. "And I take it the orb showed you something that has upset you?"

I inhaled and exhaled deeply. "Mateo. He was in a dark corridor...and Velkan and the demon wolves...trapped him." My tiny voice cracked.

Anton waited patiently as I struggled to find the words to tell him what I had seen.

Tears slid down my cheeks. "Mateo tried to take the Rose Box."

"And Velkan caught him, and he's taking him to King Calvin?"

I nodded, glad I didn't have to say it out loud.

"So now you want to rush out of Legacy and run to his aid and free him from our enemies single-handedly?"

I blinked and sat back as if he'd just slapped me hard across the face for being such a dumbass.

I lifted my chin defiantly. "Mateo's going to be tortured like Ashton."

"Perhaps. Perhaps not. Mateo is the Captain of the Royal Guard, you know, and very resourceful. However, if you run recklessly back to Iredale Palace, what do you think will happen?" His you're-being-foolish tone only made me want to prove that I wasn't.

"I'm not an idiot, Anton."

He shrugged. "I never said you were. But you're not yet strong enough to take on Velkan, the demon wolves, and King Calvin all at once. You'll only lose that beautiful head of yours."

I clenched my fists, tempted to throw the Magic Orb at him. "Then what do you suggest I do?"

"Stick with our original plan. You and Ashton will not be able to stay here much longer anyway, since King Calvin will be sending special agents to retrieve both of you, endangering my students. We need to figure out what you should do next, specifically where you should go to start reading and practicing the *Book of Goody*."

I glanced down at Ashton's pale face. "You want him to come with me? Are you sure he's strong enough?"

"He's stronger than you think. I suspect it will take Ashton, Mateo, Remi, and you to bring down the king."

Hades snarled as if saying 'don't forget about me'.

Anton tilted his head back and laughed. "Don't worry, little dragon. You know you're always part of the team, too."

Hades laid his head on my lap and looked at me with soulful eyes as I tried to process what Anton was saying.

I stared down at Ashton worriedly. "But they could all get hurt."

"Yes, they could." Anton gave me a sympathetic look. "But every war has casualties, Salem. It can't be helped. Raven and Ebony had to make these same hard choices, but they didn't take on their enemies alone. They formed teams—Raven had the Defenders, and Ebony the Sentinels. Only together were they able to conquer their enemies."

I thought of Raven and Ebony and the stories Ashton and Remi had told me about them. He was right. Neither of them had acted like the Lone Ranger.

I wiped my tears. "Fine. I'll do it your way."

He gave me a beaming smile. "Good." He squeezed my shoulder gently. "We will meet in an hour. Trust in your friends, Salem. Believe in them. They believe in you."

He quietly left us. I glanced at the orb that was still stubbornly murky and obviously wasn't going to show me Mateo again. I placed it on the nightstand and held Ashton's limp hand.

He was so still. I squeezed his hand a little. "I wish you would wake up. I need you and I don't know what to do."

I wasn't sure, but I thought I felt a squeeze back.

"Ashton?" I whispered.

His eyes fluttered open and he stared at me pleadingly. "Don't...leave...me." His voice was so weak I almost couldn't hear him.

"Dr. Greenwood, Dr. Greenwood," I called frantically.

"Salem, I'm not going to ask you again—"

"He's awake."

Dr. Greenwood's frowned turned into a smile as he came to the side of Ashton's bed. "Is he now?" He looked down at Ashton. "Finally, awake, my dear boy?"

Ashton gazed up at him with confusion and didn't answer.

Dr. Greenwood studied him carefully and then put his hand on his forehead. "I think he needs some more *clarious* elixir."

"What's that?"

"A mixture of special healing herbs from the Starlight Kingdom. I'll be right back."

Ashton cleared his throat. "I...want...I want..." His voice was so hoarse that it must have hurt him to talk.

I stared at him, wishing I could read his mind. "What? What do you want?"

But he didn't have time to answer before Dr. Greenwood returned with a glass filled with a glowing purple liquid. He gently lifted Ashton's shoulders off the pillow and brought the glass to his dry lips. "Drink this, Ashton. You'll feel better."

Ashton started to sip the purple mixture but he choked, and the liquid slipped down his chin.

Dr. Greenwood stopped, allowing Ashton to take deep breaths.

"You need to take the rest of this, Ashton. I promise you'll feel better."

Ashton nodded his head. "I can...I can...drink it myself."

The doctor cocked his eyebrow but he gave the glass to Ashton. He was shaking so bad I thought he'd spill it all over himself, but the prince surprised me. He drained the glass and handed it back to Dr. Greenwood.

"At least it tastes good," Ashton mumbled.

Dr. Greenwood stiffened. "None of my elixirs or potions tastes bad." He actually sounded hurt, as if Ashton had insulted him.

"Thank you for helping him," I said, not sure what else to say.

Ashton took a quivering breath. "Yeah. Thanks, Doc."

The Fae doctor smiled and then headed back to his back room.

I almost wanted to peek inside to see what he was doing. Was he a mad scientist, experimenting with different potions?

"Salem." Ashton struggled to sit up. "Unless I was dreaming, I think I heard you talking with Anton. If there's a meeting today, I have to be at it."

I nodded.

"You weren't dreaming, but you're not strong enough," Dr. Greenwood said firmly as he came out of the back room again.

Ashton panted as he leaned against the headboard. "Please. I... need to be...there."

"The tonic needs time to heal you." Dr. Greenwood studied him. "You're pale and you're still having trouble breathing. You don't want to pass out at the meeting, do you?"

Ashton glared. "I'm a prince, and I want to go." His you-jump-at-royalty tone wasn't working on the scowling Fae healer.

Dr. Greenwood put his hands on his hips. "So? I'm your doctor. I'll decide if you're strong enough to go the meeting —*Prince*." He emphasized the last word, eliciting a snort from Ashton.

I flashed Ashton a teasing smile. "At least his arrogance is back, Doctor. That's a good sign."

Ashton rolled his eyes and folded his arms.

Dr. Greenwood rubbed his chin. "Anton did say the meeting would concern him. Very well. I'll let you go if—"

"If what?" Ashton demanded.

"If I can go to the meeting too. If I suspect you're weakening, then we leave. End of story. Agreed?"

Ashton snorted as if the doctor had asked him to give up his crown.

I blurted. "He does."

Dr. Greenwood flashed me a look. "Very well. All of us will attend."

I glanced at the clock. "It's almost time. Is he well enough to walk?"

Ashton narrowed his eyes and threw off his covers. "I can walk." He sat up quickly, and his eyes fluttered and his face paled.

Dr. Greenwood grabbed his arm. "We move slowly. Or you're going to find yourself face down on the ground."

Ashton rubbed his forehead. "Sorry, I just sat up too fast. I'm okay now."

But his face was turning whiter by the minute. Soon, he'd be a ghost.

I held his clammy hand. "Are you sure you can walk to Anton's?"

He nodded. "Yes. I just can't go fast."

I glanced at the good doctor who shrugged. Honestly, I was glad he was coming with us. If Ashton did a nose dive, there would be no way I could lift him.

Dr. Greenwood slipped Ashton's arm around his shoulder. "Come on, let's go."

Ashton tried to pull his arm away. "I can walk."

"My way or the highway," Dr. Greenwood said grimly.

"Fine."

Together we all headed toward the door, moving at a snail's pace.

Something glimmered on the nightstand. Oh, crap. The orb. I hurried over to retrieve it and froze.

The clouds were moving again.

4

"*S*alem, what's happening?" Ashton asked warily. He looked so pale that I wasn't sure even with Dr. Greenwood's help that he could make it to the meeting.

Hades nudged my leg as if to say, 'let's go'.

I turned away from the orb that had so far only revealed moving dark clouds.

He and Dr. Greenwood were standing at the infirmary door, waiting for me.

"The orb," I frowned. "Some clouds are moving inside, but nothing is forming."

"They might resolve to something at the meeting," Dr. Greenwood said. "We need to head over now."

I hurried over to Ashton and draped his arm across my shoulders, slipping the orb into my other hand.

"I don't need any help," he murmured.

I elbowed him in the ribs softly. "Shut up."

Dr. Greenwood and I shuffled out of the infirmary, grunting and groaning. Ashton could barely walk and he was completely dead weight. We moved slowly down the steps one at a time.

Beads of sweat trickled down my forehead and ran down my temples.

Anton's quarters seemed like they were a million miles away, even though it was just across the courtyard. The muscles in my legs cramped up and I trembled, but I refused to give up and gritted my teeth.

"I'm not sure this is such a good idea," Dr. Greenwood said. "He's getting paler and paler."

Panting, I shook my head. "No...he needs to come...we can't stop now."

Footsteps ran up behind me. I glanced over my shoulder to see Lucien.

"Here. Let me." Lucien gently lifted Ashton's arm off my shoulder and onto his own.

I opened my mouth to argue, then shut it again. Stubborn or not, I had to do what was best for Ashton.

"Thanks," I mumbled.

I shoved my hair out of my eyes and followed Dr. Greenwood and Lucien to Anton's quarters. The orb still was a cloudy mess, no matter how many times I shook the damned thing like a snow globe. What was happening to Mateo?

Probably something bad.

I bit my lip, vowing not to burst into tears again. Turning into a baby wasn't going to help Mateo.

Stay cool

Anton opened his door and motioned us inside with his arm. "Bring him in here and put him on the couch."

I clutched the orb tightly as I brushed past Anton.

Ashton panted hard and laid his head back on the sofa. "I'm all right. I'm all right."

He kept saying that but his eyes fluttered shut. I sat behind and held his hand.

"We will hold the meeting here." Anton smiled. "Hopefully, Ashton won't pass out."

"I won't," Ashton mumbled, but he didn't lift up his head or open his eyes. I sat next to him and Dr. Greenwood sat on the other side.

Hades curled up at the bottom of my feet, same as always. Ashton slipped his cold, clammy hand in mine and I squeezed it gently, expecting a return grip. I was disappointed when I didn't get one.

Raven and my aunt Remi walked into the sitting room and Raven looked around curiously. "Who else is coming?" she asked.

"No one else." Anton picked up a thick leather book that was sitting on a coffee table and then sat in his red leather chair. "Raven and Remi, please, take a seat."

Lucien scooted over on the matching loveseat to give his mate room. Remi took another chair like Anton's.

"This is the *Book of Goody*." Anton held up the thick leather book. "As you all know, it's a powerful spell book, and like all such books, the spells must be learned in order. What's different about this book is that if you don't cast a spell properly, the spell will backfire on you and become a dark spell."

A wave of cold fear surged through me and I shivered.

Remi glanced over at me. "I have said this before—shouldn't Salem have a teacher?"

Anton gave her a sad look. "Normally, she would. Here at Legacy there are many professors that could help her. But Remi, as I already said, I can't afford to put my students at risk. Salem needs to learn the spells on her own."

Remi narrowed her eyes. "That's ridiculous. Just where do you think she should go?"

"You mean all of you," Anton corrected.

Remi threw up her hands. "Fine, all of us. Again, where, pray tell?"

"I have a cabin that is forty miles north of here that I have used as a retreat before. It's very secure and well hidden."

Raven's eyes widened. "Really? I didn't know you had a secret cabin."

Anton gave her a solemn smile. "Then it wouldn't be much of a secret, would it?"

"Is it warded?" Remi asked.

"Yes. And I have a caretaker there that guards it for me. He's name is Quint. He's a fellow vampire and I have sent word to him to expect visitors soon," Anton said. "Even though my cabin is well warded, I'm afraid Calvin's witch will be able to find it eventually."

Remi crossed her arms. "Then we shouldn't go there."

"Wherever you go," Anton said, "this witch would be able to find you. It's only a matter of time. My cabin's as good a place as anywhere to lie low until Salem learns the spells."

He made it sound like I would be able to master magic in just a couple of days. Somehow, I didn't think it worked that way. I needed help. I thought of Hayley trapped in that cage and an idea popped into my head.

I cleared my throat. "I have a radical idea. I need teacher. What if I rescued the witch Hayley?"

"You mean we," Ashton mumbled. I ignored him.

"Hayley is under Calvin's command." Anton's eyes darkened and he tapped his fingers on the armrest. "It would be extremely dangerous."

"Then we shouldn't do it." Remi held my gaze. "There has to be another way."

"Okay," I said. "What do you think we should do?"

Remi gave me a don't-take-that-tone-with-me glare. "I don't know yet. That's why we're having this meeting."

I turned to Anton. "Is it possible to free Hayley?"

Anton didn't answer me right away. After a few long minutes, he asked, "Are you sure this isn't just a ploy to get back to Iredale Palace so you can rescue Mateo?"

"I don't know," I said honestly. "Subconsciously, maybe.

Maybe not. But that book could be really dangerous. I don't want to hurt anyone if I use the wrong spell. Hayley might be my best hope."

"Anton, do you think Hayley could help Salem master her abilities?" Raven asked.

"It doesn't matter," Remi interrupted. "I won't...I can't...risk Calvin getting his hands on Salem like he did my sister and brother-in-law. She's not strong enough to face him...not yet, anyway."

Raven stared at Anton. "Well?"

"Hayley's a witch," he eventually said slowly. "She could help her."

I frowned. "Only *could*?"

"Don't forget, Hayley's the one who helped Calvin murder your parents."

"I know," I said. "But I heard she didn't have a choice."

"We all have choices," Anton countered.

I didn't like where this was going. "What do you mean?"

"Simple. She could have forfeited her life to save her parents, but instead, she chose to sacrifice your parents to save her own skin." His crisp voice crushed any hope I had of trusting Hayley.

I battled back tears that were again threatening to fall. "So you're saying she could betray me like she did my parents?"

He nodded. "Yes."

"Mateo trusts her," Ashton croaked, lifting his head off the back of the couch as if it weighed a hundred pounds.

Not sure if I heard him right, I looked at him. "He trusts her? Are you sure?"

He nodded. "Yeah, I am."

Suddenly, something felt warm in my hand and I opened up my palm to look. The dark clouds in the orb had finally parted.

"No." I lost the battle with the tears.

Remi hurried over to me. "Honey, what's wrong?"

I took a deep, steadying breath to stop the tears turning from a trickle into a torrent. "Mateo. He's in Calvin's secret room and... and he's being tortured." My voice shattered.

Just like Ashton had been earlier, Mateo was strung up in chains, half naked, dangling like a piece of meat. Bloody lashes covered his battered torso and his handsome face was swollen, turning a million shades of black and blue.

Anton came over to me and peered into the orb. "There must be a reason Calvin is keeping him alive. Anyone that Calvin considers to be traitor has always been killed."

"Bait," Ashton whispered.

My gut tightened. "If I don't come, he'll hurt him more, won't he?"

"You know he will." Anton returned to his chair. "He's hoping you'll rush in alone like an impetuous fool."

"I won't, but I can't let Mateo die either."

Remi clasped my cheeks. "You can't go back to Iredale Palace. It's a trap."

"Gloria," Ashton murmured. "She can help."

Remi dropped her hands and stared at him. "Are you insane? Calvin's daughter? She'll turn on us at the drop of a hat."

I thought about that. "Actually, I don't think that's true. She'd do anything to save Ashton."

"But that's Ashton," Remi pointed out. "Not Mateo. Why would she risk her life to save a guard, especially one that betrayed her father?"

Shit. Our odds were getting worse, not better. I had to trust two women that I barely knew, knowing if they betrayed me, more people could get hurt or even die. I was cornered with no clear idea of which path to choose.

Ashton wiped the sweat off his brow with his arm. "I think she will. Gloria doesn't have many allies, but Mateo's one of them. She'll help him. I believe in her."

Remi laughed bitterly. "My god, you're trusting Calvin's

daughter." Tears glistened in her eyes and she rubbed the bridge of her nose. "It's Libby all over again."

My heart dropped at her words. I met her fearful gaze. "Remi, I don't like these choices either, but I don't think we have many others."

"We can hide you," she said. "Until you're strong enough to face your uncle."

I gave her a sad smile. "Remi, haven't you been listening? I can't do this alone. I need help in learning how to use the *Book of Goody*."

Anton tapped his index finger on the leather book. "I really do believe that's the key to Salem defeating her uncle."

Remi glared. "If this is true, why don't you send Salem one of your teachers?"

Anton sighed heavily. "I think you know the answer to that. If I did, Calvin would consider it an act of war. Do you really think we're ready for another supernatural war? Because personally, I don't."

Remi hung her head. "You're right. I don't either."

I looked at everyone's faces. "So...what do we now?"

"If I'm not mistaken," Raven looked at me, "I think you, Remi, and Ashton are all going to be riding the Silver Dragon Express to Anton's secret cabin."

"I think that's best. I wish I could do more." Anton got up and handed the *Book of Goody* to me.

The minute I touched the leather cover, tingles ran over my fingers, rushing up my arms and down my back, making shiver. I snatched my hand away.

Anton looked at me sharply. "You felt the magic, didn't you?"

"I did." I studied the book, afraid to even open it. The magic in it was strong, very strong. It wasn't something I was sure I could manage.

Anton returned to his seat. "The *Book of Goody* is yours now.

33

Use it wisely. Rushing through it will only bring you and others around you harm."

"I understand."

More strange sensations pumped through me as I felt a strong invisible force pulling on me, compelling me to use the book.

It terrified me.

5

*M*y heart quickened as the *Book of Goody* practically shook itself open in my lap. I thought about shoving it aside, but I couldn't bring myself to do it.

Anton looked at each of us. "Meeting adjourned." He stood. "Salem and Remi, you should grab any belongings that you think you'll need. I haven't been to my cabin for some time and don't have any clothes there for you."

"What about food?" Remi asked.

"As I have said, Quint knows you'll coming and he'll have the cabin fully stocked for you. If you require anything further, there's a general store nearby in the town of Silver Stone."

Dr. Greenwood, who had been silent for the entire meeting, rubbed his chin. "I'm not sure Ashton is well enough to travel, even by dragon."

Ashton gritted his teeth. "I'm going."

I squeezed Ashton's hand gently. "Dr. Greenwood, I promise that Remi and I will take good care of him."

Dr. Greenwood frowned. "I suppose I'm not going to have a say in this matter, am I?" He wasn't looking at me. He was focusing on Anton.

"I'm afraid not, Dr. Greenwood," Anton said. "Can you send something with Salem to help Ashton? He seems to be healing."

"If I must—" Dr. Greenwood's low tone was less than happy.

"Yes. You must," Anton said firmly.

The doctor stood. "I will prepare some tonics and potions for Ashton." He gave the prince a long, hard stare. "But he must stay in bed for at least a week." He wagged his finger sternly. "No exceptions."

Remi folded her arms. "Don't worry. He'll stay in bed, even if I have to sit on him."

Ashton gave her a I'd-like-to-see-you-try look but wisely kept his mouth shut.

"Good," Dr. Greenwood said. He seemed satisfied at last, and left the meeting to return to the infirmary.

Hades woke when people got up. He yawned and stretched out his paws, arching his back like a cat.

Anton headed down the hallway. "Raven and Lucien, please come with me. I'll show you where you're going but I must insist you keep its location secret."

"We will. Don't worry," Lucien mumbled.

Of course Lucien was going to come with us. Raven was lucky. Not many people had the love that those two shared.

Remi headed for the front door. "I'm going to get us some clothes."

I frowned. "Clothes? Where?"

"I'm going to have one of the Barons go to the outlet stores and buy us some things."

My eyes widened. "There's an outlet store?"

"Yes, in Silverthorne. I don't think it's safe for us to go shopping ourselves. Is there anything special you want?"

I shrugged. "Not really." Clothes shopping had never been big on my to do list since I couldn't afford it. Once again, I felt like a beggar with no money.

Remi winked. "Then I'll surprise you."

Ashton glowered. "I'm not staying in bed for a week. I'm not an invalid."

I laid my head on the back of couch and looked into his eyes that he was trying to keep open. "Nobody said you were, Ashton, but Calvin tortured you. You need time to recover."

"It wasn't just physical torture, you know." He lifted the back of his hand and caressed my cheek. "He used magic."

I scowled. "But Calvin can't use magic."

"I know."

I sucked in a breath. "He made Hayley do it?"

Sadness flickered in his eyes. "Yes. She didn't want to, begged Calvin to stop compelling her. But he wouldn't. She cried when she saw she was hurting me." His voice was weary, as if just remembering it all weighed heavily on him.

Anger smoldered inside me. "Why didn't you say anything during the meeting? There's no way I can trust Hayley if she did that."

"Salem, don't judge her. She didn't want to. She's a prisoner, just like I was. I didn't trust her at first either...but Mateo does." He dropped his hand and closed his eyes. "And I trust him."

My anger lessened but I was still on edge. Was she torturing Mateo just like she had Ashton?

I squeezed his hand. "Ashton, what exactly did Hayley do to you?"

He didn't answer me right away.

"She made the pain worse and prevented the wounds from healing."

I gasped. "Oh my God. That's horrible."

"Yes, but she could have done worse. Much worse."

Uneasiness fluttered in my gut, but I didn't ask any more questions. Ashton fell asleep and began to snore softly.

I couldn't help but wonder what kind of spells were in the Book of Goody. Were there evil ones as well as good? I shuddered.

I didn't think I could use a spell to hurt someone—well, maybe Calvin.

Hades got up and sniffed at the book. He released a low growl, as if he felt its power.

I rubbed his head. "Easy, boy."

But he kept eying the book suspiciously as I slowly opened it to take a peek inside. The paper was thick and wrinkled, reminding me of paper mache, and the text wasn't printed, it was hand painted with thick letters. There were also symbols— symbols I didn't understand. That was definitely a problem. If I didn't know what they meant, could I cast some evil spell without even knowing it?

I flipped the papers, looking for an index or footnotes that would explain the strange symbols, but I didn't see anything.

Anton entered the living room.

I immediately closed the book, my cheeks heating. I felt like I had been caught peeking at Christmas presents. I blurted, "Um, where are Raven and Lucien?"

"Packing." He gave me a warm smile. "Salem, if you have any questions about the book, now is the time to ask."

I brushed my hand over the thick leather cover. "Umm. There's some strange symbols and I don't know what they mean."

"Interesting. I thought maybe Remi would have explained those to you, but I forget—it's your mother that possessed the power, not your aunt." He motioned with his hand. "Come with me to my study."

I slid the book onto the cushion next to Ashton.

"Hades, stay with Ashton."

He whined but did as he was told and lay down next to Ashton.

I ruffled his mane. "Thanks, buddy."

I got to my feet and followed Anton down the hallway. He led me into his study where he had so many books that it was like walking into a library. Not that I had been in many libraries—libraries equaled boredom to me.

I headed over to a bookcase that had volumes with strange writing on the spines.

Anton came up behind me. "Those are written in the ancient Fae language. It isn't used anymore."

"You mean like Latin?"

"Something like that." He handed me a thick book. "Here. I think this will help."

The black leather book was heavy. It had stars circling around a moon on the cover and underneath in bold letters was written *Ancient Symbols of Spellcasting*. "What is this?"

He placed a hand on my shoulder gently. "Think of it as a magical dictionary for petroglyphs."

"So, it will help me learn about the symbols in the Book of Goody?"

"Yes. Given that you have no knowledge of the magical symbols, I suggest you study this first before you attempt to use any spells. You must be absolutely certain what the petroglyphs in the *Book of Goody* mean before you use them."

I sighed heavily. "Because if I don't, the spell may backfire?"

"Yes."

I rubbed my forehead. "I'm really not sure I can do this. I was never good in school."

Anton gave me a solemn stare. "Believe me, Salem. You are the Chosen one. Only you can free your people, people who are not only under the control of a brutal dictator but also shrouded in a veil of dark magic."

"I didn't think that Hayley practiced dark magic."

"She doesn't. But King Calvin is aligned with the Unseelie and they do."

"But I thought all the Unseelie were banished back to the Elder Dimension."

"Not all—most. Some of the Unseelie escaped. And unfortunately Calvin has continued his alliance with the Unseelie, even though he firmly denies it."

"Why don't you all just call him on it?" I couldn't hide the frustration in my voice.

"To accuse a king, you must have definite proof, and that's something we don't have. The Unseelie deny they are aligned with him as well. And then there's also the demons from hell, who are twice as powerful."

Suddenly, I felt very small and very weak. "You really think I'm strong enough to take all these forces on?"

"The first King of the Moon Kingdom was very powerful, not only as a wolf but as a witch."

I wrinkled my brow. "I thought only women were witches."

"Both men and women can be witches. If you're thinking of warlocks, they practice the dark arts."

"Does Calvin have any magical abilities?"

"No, but he's enslaved Hayley and forced her to serve him. He has them by proxy."

I thumbed through the book of ancient symbols, looking at the strange stick figures. Some of them looked so similar that it would be easy to mix them up. He was right, I had to learn these first. I looked up from the dictionary. "Will the *Book of Goody* have a spell that will break Haley's enslavement?"

"Perhaps, but it would be very powerful and deplete your energy enormously. And if you didn't perform it correctly, things could go terribly, terribly wrong."

"That's comforting," I grumbled.

"Remember, you won't be taking all of them on by yourself. If you tried, it could be disastrous."

I thought of Ashton and Mateo. "I just don't like the idea of anyone getting hurt because of me."

"I know." Sorrow flashed in his eyes. "None of us do."

A lump formed in my throat knowing I would soon have to

depart Legacy Academy. It was the first place in the last couple of weeks that I had felt safe. "So, when do we leave?"

"Tonight. You need to fly under the cover of darkness. If Calvin has spies in the forest, they will be able to spot all of you otherwise."

"But I thought Raven could camouflage all of us. She did at Iredale Palace."

"Yes, but she can't hide all of you. Plus, I suspect that Calvin may have come up with a spell that could counter Raven's."

As usual Calvin was one step ahead of us. I could practically feel his foul breath on the back of my neck.

"Come." He headed out of the study. "We will have one last meal together before you leave."

I clutched the ancient book to my chest. "Anton, if Calvin can track me here, won't he be able to find me at your cabin?"

Back in the living room, Ashton and Hades were both sleeping soundly. "My cabin is well warded. It will take some time before he'll be able to do that."

I shivered. "But he'll be able to eventually?"

"Unfortunately, yes. It's only a matter of time. But don't worry —it won't happen overnight, especially since he doesn't know my cabin even exists." His confident voice did nothing to dispel my doubts.

Deciphering these two spell books would take time—time I didn't have.

6

*a*fter a fabulous dinner of assorted deep-dish pizzas and Caesar salad, it was time to leave for Anton's cabin. I sat at the dining room table staring sadly at the empty pizza pans and salad bowls, wishing for all the world I could stay here. Legacy Academy was definitely a magical place and I could see why Raven felt like this had been her home.

But I didn't have the luxury of staying, thanks to my uncle.

Raven looked at me and smiled. "Are you ready to fly dragon style again?"

I took a deep breath and slid my plate away. "I guess so."

"My cabin is actually very nice," said Anton reassuringly. "I think you'll like it. Quint, the caretaker, takes really good care of it."

"I'm sure he does," I mumbled.

"Thanks for allowing us to stay there." Remi finished off the last bit of her red wine. "I'm not sure where else we could have gone, since Calvin has discovered every one of our secret hiding places."

Anton patted his lips with a napkin. "As I have said before, Calvin will track you to my cabin eventually, but it won't be for a while yet. My cabin will hide Salem's scent for a time, though."

Ugh. Whenever anyone used that word, I always felt like I had a serious case of body odor.

I picked up my plate to take it back to the kitchen, but Anton shook his head.

"Cook will take care of the dishes," he said. "It's time for you to leave."

I glumly put back the plate, feeling like he was kicking us all out.

"If I do overthrow my uncle, then will I be able to attend an academy? Maybe even this one?"

Say yes Say yes Say yes

Anton held my gaze. "I'm sorry, Salem, but I don't think so. You'll have a kingdom to run by then. But your staff and advisors will teach you how to be a good and gentle queen."

"That's not the same thing as attending an academy," I grumbled.

"Sacrifices are always made with rulers." He gave me a sad smile. "Nothing is ever simple."

Not what I wanted to hear.

"But I do have something for you." He retrieved a Legacy Academy backpack from the kitchen. "This is for you to remember us by."

I swallowed hard, refusing to cry. "Thank you." I don't think he realized how much this simple gift meant to me. Or maybe he did. He was Anton, after all.

"You're welcome." He looked at each one of us. "Finish up any last-minute packing you have. It's time to go."

"I'll be right back." I clutched the backpack and hurried back to my bedroom and looked around it one last time.

The red canopy bed, matching leather chair, and hand-carved mahogany furniture were so beautiful that they had made me feel like I really was a princess, but here I was being forced to move yet again. My sword was on the leather chair and the moonstones in the handle glittered. I put on my belt and secured the sword in its sheath. The power in the sword made it tremble against my thigh, making me break out in goosebumps.

I grabbed the two spell books and the magic orb and carefully put them in my new backpack. I wiggled my arms into the straps and headed out the door. The books pressed against my back and I wasn't sure if it was my imagination or not, but I thought tingles ran up and down my spine. It was almost as if the *Book of Goody*— or maybe it was the magic orb—was alive.

Whatever happened, I was ready for battle.

Everyone was in the living room waiting for me. Ashton had his hand on the back of the sofa, and he was gripping it so hard, his knuckles were turning white. He was having a hard time not falling over. He glanced at my backpack. "Do you want me to carry that?"

"No, I've got it."

Anton picked up two small glass jars with glowing liquid inside from the coffee table. Once was green and the other blue. "Dr. Greenwood wanted me to give these to you, Salem. They're special healing potions for Ashton. He said Ashton is supposed to have a sip, just a sip, of each one every day. He mustn't drink all of it at once, or he could slip into a coma. May I put them in your backpack?"

"Of course."

I turned and he unzipped my backpack and tucked the containers inside.

"Follow me," he said.

He led us up to the balcony off his bedroom that looked over the Legacy grounds. Moonlight peeked through the thick branches of the pines and aspens, and a flock of geese flew across the sky. Soft lights illuminated the towers that had flags flying at the top of the turrets, representing the various supernatural races— Golden Demon, wolf, dragon, vampire, and Fae. It was late and students were back in their towers, either studying or sleeping. How I wished I was one of the wolf students, studying for my classes the next day.

Up on the balcony, our waiting suitcases had been filled with brand new clothes from the factory outlet stores. I should have been excited, but honestly I'd rather have a closet full of uniforms for here.

"It's time for everyone to leave," Anton said quietly. "Lucien, you and Hades will fly behind Raven just in case Calvin has anticipated our plan and has sent a small army to intercept you."

Crap, this again. Someone else was going to get hurt because of me, I just knew it.

I scowled. "How can we take on a small army and win?"

Lucien gave me a smirk. "I'm tougher than you think." He scratched Hades' ear. "Besides, this guy puts fear even in the toughest Unseelie."

"I'm no slouch either," Raven said as she quickly stripped off her clothes and then shifted into her magnificent silver dragon.

The moonlight glistened off her scales, making it look like she was glowing. Against the night sky she would shine like a beacon, but day or night it would be hard to hide a dragon almost the size of a Mac truck.

Raven turned her head and nodded toward her back as if to say, 'hop on'.

Ashton wobbled on first and wrapped his arms around her thick neck.

I stretched out my arm. "You next, Remi."

"I can ride behind you two," she said.

I put my hand on my chest, trying to keep my thundering heart from popping out in between my ribs. "No, I'll go in the back. Please."

Remi reluctantly scooted up behind Ashton.

"Good luck, Salem." Anton patted me on the back. "Remember, you're not alone in this. Trust your friends."

I nodded, but I was tired of people getting hurt because of me and I was worried. I climbed on the dragon's broad back and sat behind Remi, hugging her. Raven stretched out her wings and lifted up into the air. Hovering, she grabbed up our luggage with her talons, then soared away high above Legacy Academy.

Anton waved goodbye from below. A hollow pit formed in my gut as Legacy fell away into the distance. For the millionth time, I wished I could have been a student there. I wanted to have tight relationships like the ones Raven had formed here, not just with Lucien, but with the Defenders. But according to everyone, that wasn't my destiny.

Hades and Lucien lunged into the clear midnight sky. Cold air whistled over me and I hung onto Remi tightly, burying my face against her shoulder.

Hades came up alongside Raven's left and I couldn't help but smile.

We flew so high up that the trees and meadows looked like toys. Calvin's spies would have to have great binoculars to spot us. My hair flapped around my face and I was constantly spitting strands of it out of my mouth The icy wind froze my fingers and seeped into my skin. I felt like I was slowly turning into an iceberg.

Several hours later, the darkness and the stars began to fade and the clouds turned pink and orange. It was dawn when Raven made her descent and the pines and aspens became larger. My attention was caught by what Anton had called a cabin. It wasn't anything of the sort—more like a stone fortress, or a castle.

A curtain wall surrounded the red title turrets and towers, and as we drew closer, I realized there were outer and inner walls protecting the fortress as well. There was only one way in, and that was via a drawbridge that could be lowered over a roaring river that surrounded the place.

With all these barriers protecting it, unwanted visitors would have a hard time getting in. No wonder Anton sent us here.

Raven landed in the middle of a stone courtyard that had a large pine tree that would offer shade on hot summer days, and stone flower beds that must be beautiful in the spring time.

I sucked in a breath. Someone was standing in the shadows of the courtyard. If this was Quint, he wasn't what I pictured at all. I was expecting a stuffy butler, like the Barons that took care of the towers at Legacy Academy. With his broad shoulders, leather pants and sword strapped to his hips, this guy looked more like a warrior. A grumpy warrior.

As Raven, Hades, and Lucien landed, the man approached us. His long curly hair flared over his shoulders and he had a beard and mustache, but it was his dark green eyes that really drew me to his ruggedly handsome face.

Lucien drew his sword and Hades stood next to him, snarling.

"Who are you?" Lucien demanded suspiciously.

"I'm Quint Dimir, the caretaker of Scarwood Fortress."

I slid off Raven's back and came up next to Hades. "You're the caretaker?"

He frowned. "Yes. Why?"

Lucien blurted, "You don't look like any caretaker to me."

Quint chuckled. "You were expecting a little old man?"

"Something like that," Lucien said as he sheathed his sword again.

I studied him, not sure I trusted him and slowly went for my weapon. "How do we know you're not working for Calvin?"

Quint's eyes turned dark red. "Because I'm a vampire, not a wolf."

I lifted up my chin high. "He has vampires working for him as well."

"True, but I'm not one of them. Look, if you don't trust me, you can leave. Up to you." He headed back toward a wooden door that led into the keep, almost daring us to follow him.

Raven had shifted into a human and was quickly getting dressed. "Well, what should we do?"

Lucien shrugged. "Follow him. I don't think we have much choice."

"It could be a trap," Ashton said. He stood slowly. He still looked like he could topple over any minute.

Shivering, I shoved my fingers through my tangled hair. "I think Lucien's right. We don't have any other place to go."

Each of us brought in a bag that Remi had packed and climbed up the steps that Quint had taken. Lucien reached the door first and silently mouthed 'on three'.

My heart roared in my ears. God, he thought we were walking into an ambush. I clutched my sword, thinking about the last time I faced a vampire.

Lucien burst through the door and we all quickly rushed inside, our weapons at the ready, but then the joke was on us. We found ourselves in a kitchen with every modern convenience, from a Kitchen Aid mixer, to two ovens, to a gas stove. Quint was frying bacon.

I inhaled the fragrant scent of coffee and my mouth watered.

He cocked his eyebrow. "Seriously? You always come armed for breakfast?"

I lowered my sword. "Breakfast?"

Quint met my gaze. "I assumed you might be hungry. If not, I'll throw it out."

Hades licked his lips and whined loudly, making me grin.

My stomach grumbled, and I gave Quint a tight smile as I sheathed my sword. "No, please don't."

"Good." He returned to frying the bacon. "Scrambled eggs and hash browns are already in the silver chafing dishes. Coffee's in the urn. Help yourself to whatever you want."

We all looked at each other. Lucien clearly wasn't satisfied and slowly went into the living room still holding his sword. Definitely not the trusting type, but then again, he'd just been through a supernatural war and my wonderful uncle was on the wrong side.

Lucien returned. "I checked out the living room and there's no one here. I swear it's decorated like Dracula lives here."

Raven grinned and draped her arms around his neck. "You're surprised?"

Lucien's frown disappeared as he stared into her eyes. "No, I guess not."

I slipped off my backpack and put the strap over a chair. My teeth wouldn't stop chattering and the tips of my hair had frosted over. "I don't know about you guys, but I need some coffee."

Ashton slid into one of the chairs. He looked even more disheveled and pale. Sweat was trickling down his temples. "I'll take some." But his voice was barely audible and his eyes were fluttering shut.

Quint frowned and pointed with the fork he was using to turn the bacon. "What's wrong with him? He doesn't look too good."

I reached into my backpack to get the potions, then looked up in alarm when I heard a noise. "Ashton!"

He had tumbled out of the chair and onto the hardwood floor.

I rushed over to him and gently slapped his face. "Ashton, Ashton, wake up."

Raven knelt next to me. "Maybe he shouldn't have come."

I put my palm over his nose. "Oh, my God. He's not breathing."

Shit, it was happening again. Someone was dying and it was all my fault.

"Get out of the way." Quint rushed over and hauled into Ashton his arms. He carried him to a nearby couch.

Quint frowned. "His heart's not beating. What the hell happened on the way over here?"

Raven gasped. "I don't know. He was clinging to my neck, and I could feel his heart beating against me then."

"It has to be the spell. We should have left him with Dr. Greenwood." Remi knelt next to Ashton, brushing his hair.

Hades sniffed and whined pitifully, as if he knew Ashton was dying.

NoNoNoNoNoNoNo

My heart jumped into panic mode. I grabbed my backpack and pulled out Dr. Greenwood's potions.

"He's not going to die." I slipped my arm around Ashton's shoulders and lifted up his head. "Ashton, can you hear me? You need to drink this."

But his frozen lips didn't open. I tried pouring the potion into his mouth but the glowing liquid just ran down his cheeks.

"Damn it. This isn't working. What am I doing wrong?"

Raven clutched my shoulder. "I think Remi's right, Salem. Somehow the dark magic is overpowering him."

I jerked my head up. "Then you need to take him back to Legacy. He can't die. He just can't." My voice was a desperate squeal.

"Calm down, Salem." She squeezed gently. "I would never make it back to Legacy in time. You have to save him."

My eyes widened. "Me? I'm not a healer."

"But some of your ancestors were witches. You have their blood in your veins." She tilted her head. "Use the *Book of Goody*. You're the only one who can save him."

They all looked at me expectantly, waiting for me to pull a rabbit out of my backpack and save the day.

7

*E*ven Raven's faith in me didn't boost my confidence. I had never done magic. What if I screwed up? Anton said for me to start with simple spells, and healing somebody didn't sound simple to me.

I gently laid Ashton's lifeless body onto the sofa, not sure if I should use the spell book or not. Anton said if I didn't go in order the spell could backfire. What if I killed him?

Remi came in with my backpack and unzipped it. "You're the only one who can save him. You have to try."

"This fucking sucks," I murmured as I pulled out the leather book.

"You have to hurry." Lucien put his palm on Ashton's forehead. "He's burning up. I don't think he's going to last much longer."

Raven frowned. "The spell must have been like a time release or something like that. See if there's something in the book about time release spells."

"I don't know, guys," I mumbled as I opened the book. "Anton really stressed I had to go in order, or the spell could backfire. I could kill him if I get it wrong."

"If you don't try," Lucien said, "he'll die. The choice is yours."

I glanced over at Ashton, his face even paler, beads of sweat dripping down his face. Whatever the spell was, it was playing havoc with his insides. Damn Hayley! What had she done to him?

Trust me. Put your hand on me and let me guide you.

"Who said that?" I whirled around, searching all of their confused faces. Even Hades tilted his head, as if to say, 'what the hell'?

Remi's brows furrowed and she looked at me strangely. "No one said anything, Salem."

"No, I just heard someone say for me to put my hand on them and let them guide me." I stared at Quint. "Was it you? Or is there someone else here?"

He folded his arms. "You're hearing things."

"Crap." I shoved my fingers through my hair. "Maybe I am going crazy."

No, you're not. Trust in me.

Tingling sensations ran up my arm, making the hairs on the back of my neck stand straight up. Then I looked down. "Oh, God," I mumbled. "I think...I think it's the book."

Raven motioned toward the book with her hand. "Anton said it was a powerful spell book." She smiled. "But don't worry. He never would have given it to you if he didn't think you could handle it."

"You're the lost princess," my aunt said. "You have to try. There's a legend that the first king was able to heal people. You have his eyes. Maybe you inherited that ability too."

"But what if I didn't?" I looked at Ashton desperately. He was getting worse. I couldn't just stand here fretting like a Wishy-Washy Wendy. I had to do something. I took a deep breath and closed the book.

"What are you doing? He's dying." Quint's voice was harsh.

The only answer was to trust the voice. I spread my palm over the cover and strange sensations began to move through my fingers. A gentle warm wind rustled around me, twirling my hair around my cheeks. I heard people gasp, but I ignored them. I had to focus. Power swept through me as an invisible force pulled on my hand. Before I knew what was happening, my fingers did the walking and then suddenly stopped on a page that had the words *Illumiicus Honorulus* written across it. Unfortunately, it was not one of the first spells and was about a quarter way through the book.

Shitshitshitshit

God, should I use it?

I glanced at Raven who gave me an encouraging nod.

"*Illumiicus Honorulus,*" I whispered.

Tingling sensations pumped through me. Pink swirls swished around my hand and shimmering sparkles drifted over toward Ashton. The sparkles divided again and again until they covered his still body like a blanket, then slowly sank down into his flesh.

I bit my lip, not sure whether I had healed or hurt my friend.

No one talked.

No one moved.

No one breathed.

Come on, Ashton. Live. I need you.

But nothing happened.

I slumped down onto my knees and tears slid down my cheeks. "Ashton...I'm so sorry."

Hades nudged his face against mine. I dropped the book and wrapped my arms around his neck, burying my face into his thick mane, hiding my tears. Anton was wrong. I wasn't powerful. I was failure.

Someone gently touched my back. "It's not your fault it didn't work," Raven said softly. "It's Calvin's. It was the work of dark magic." Her words only turned up the waterworks and I clutched Hades tighter, crying harder and harder.

"I'll take him to one of the rooms upstairs," Quint said. "Who was he?"

"Prince Ashton Shaw of the Tundra Kingdom." Lucien sat

heavily in a chair as if he were defeated. "He was King Christopher's only son."

Quint grunted but didn't say a word as he carried Ashton's lifeless body up the stairs.

I released Hades abruptly and wiped my sweaty palms on my thighs. "Excuse me. I need to be alone." I got up abruptly and headed out into the courtyard.

The cold air was crisp and froze the tears to my cheeks. I couldn't face anyone in there. We shouldn't have brought Ashton with us, no matter how badly he wanted to come. Dr. Greenwood could have saved him. I was fucking useless.

Shivering, I sat on the steps that led into the castle and hugged my knees to my chest. Everyone thought I was like the first king, but time and time again, I'd proven I wasn't. Why did people keep believing in me?

The door opened. I didn't look over my shoulder to see who it was. I didn't care.

"Leave me alone." My harsh voice came out loud and clear. In the foster homes where I grew up, that tone had always been enough to keep nosey foster parents or goody two-shoes social workers away from me.

Not so today. Hades plopped down next to me and laid his head on my lap, and Raven sat next to me and handed me a steaming cup of coffee. "Here."

I thought about storming off for a split second but then graciously took the cup that warmed my stiff fingers. "Thank you."

She rubbed my back. At first I stiffened, but then I slowly relaxed. No one had ever comforted me when I was growing up in foster care, and I had to admit her gentle touch helped.

"I know what it's like to lose someone, remember."

I bit my lip. "You mean Bo?"

She nodded. "I had been weakened in battle, all my energy drained, and Ryker was coming for me. Bo stepped in front of me, taking the full force of Ryker's dark magic. I tried to draw on my magic to save him, but…" She cleared her throat. "I couldn't."

"Where were the Defenders?"

She didn't answer right away and took a long sip of her coffee. "Fighting elsewhere. Lucien couldn't get to us in time. I didn't just lose Bo that night—I also lost Poppy, one of my best friends. She died protecting the wolf she loved—Xavier."

"How did you get through it?"

"At first, I didn't. After the battle, I stayed with my best friend Julie and her family. She's the one that pulled me out of my depression." She took a shaky breath. "And now she's gone too."

"Julie? I never heard of her."

"We were best friends since elementary school. We were inseparable." She gave me a sarcastic smile. "Until I became a dragon. Then everything changed."

"What happened to her? Did Ryker or Cormac kill her too?"

She shook her head. "No. She died in a drag race, trying to impress some stupid guy."

"That's awful. I'm so sorry."

"The funny thing is, now she's a reaper."

My eyes widened. "Seriously? A reaper? They exist?"

"Yup. But don't worry, she doesn't have a skeleton face or anything like that. She's still Julie, she just reaps souls now. She even has a mate who's another reaper, Rusty. They both work for the Archangel Michael."

"Wow. That totally blows my brain away."

She laughed. "I know, right?" Then her eyes turned serious. "Julie had problems with Velkan and the demon wolves, same as you."

My heart stilled. "What happened?"

"She inadvertently sold her soul to the demon Balthazar and he sent the wolves after her."

"Balthazar?"

"Yeah, a demon from Hell. Balthazar's directly under Satan.

And no, he's got nothing to do with the Golden Demons or even the Dark Demons. Totally different races."

"So what happened when the demon wolves came after her?"

"She and the Gargoyles—that's her team—defeated them and she won her soul back." She held my gaze. "I'm telling you this because those wolves were definitely under some kind of spell. Julie could sense it when she fought them. You'll have to break it."

I tipped my head back and laughed bitterly. "Raven, have you seen my track record on casting spells? I'm sure I'll be no better at breaking them. You're betting on the wrong horse."

She patted my thigh. "No. I'm not. It takes time, Salem. It took me four years to master my powers."

My chest tightened. "But you went to an academy. I can't do that."

"I know. But you've got people who can help you. You have to trust in them."

"I have one fewer now." Sadness crept into my voice.

"When Bo died, his brother, Zayne, took his place on the Defenders. He's now the king of the Ember Kingdom. You may find someone to replace Ashton."

I nodded, but a huge lump plugged my throat and I couldn't answer. How could I replace Ashton? He wasn't replaceable. And what if the same thing was happening to Mateo even now?

War sucked.

The door creaked open again.

"There's something coming." Quint's grim voice broke the moment between Raven, Hades, and I.

Raven stood and frowned. "What is it?"

He shrugged. "I don't know, but Lucien's gone out to investigate."

"Damn it." Raven rushed into the castle.

I looked down at Hades. "Go protect Lucien, little buddy."

Hades didn't hesitate. He spread his wings and soared out of the courtyard.

"Come back," I whispered. "Both of you."

I couldn't lose either of them, especially Hades. My heart couldn't take it.

What if Calvin had somehow discovered our plans? What if he had spies? Maybe even spies at Legacy?

8

Quint drew his sword and opened the door to the keep. "Follow me to the guard tower."

He was twice as tall as me and I had to race to keep up with him. He tore open a wooden door to reveal a winding spiral staircase with flickering torches.

Clomp Clomp Clomp

His heavy footsteps pounded on the stone steps and my heavy panting breaths as I tried to keep up echoed off the walls.

He went through an open door that led to a round turret from which I could see for miles and miles. The wind blew around us, whirling like a mini tornado and tossing my hair around my face. Raven and Remi were already there. The thick pines and aspens made it difficult to see if there was any movement below. So far only the tree branches flittered under the wind.

"I don't see them. Where are they?" Panic crept into Raven's voice. She pulled on the hem of her sweater.

But Quinton frowned. "I wouldn't shift if I were you. There aren't many dragons around here, especially a silver one, and you'll be sounding the alarm that you're here."

She puffed out a whip of air. "But Hades and Lucien—"

"Can take care of themselves."

"How do you know?" she asked warily.

Admiration flared in his eyes. "Even in this neck of the woods, Lucien's and Hades' reputations are legendary, same as yours."

"Look!" Remi pointed. "Something's flying through the trees."

Hades burst out of the trees first, heading straight for us. Lucien was right behind him and seemed to have someone clinging to his neck, but I couldn't tell who it was.

Aaaaaaooo Aaaaaooo Aaaaaooo

Angry howls hit me like a brick wall. My shoulders slumped. "Shit, the demon wolves found us."

"But they won't be able to tell anyone about it." Quint hopped on top of the wall and then jumped.

"Quint," I yelled. "No."

But he spread his arms wide and shifted into the biggest black bat I had ever seen. I swear he was as big as a horse.

"How did he do that?" I gasped. "He didn't take off his clothes or anything."

"Vampires aren't shifters," Raven said. "Their abilities are different than ours. They don't have to remove their clothes to change into their bat."

I never knew that. I guess in the movies they never took their clothes off to change into a bat, but then again, I didn't put much faith in Hollywood since most of the time they got everything wrong.

Quint flew past Hades and Lucien and descended into the thick forest.

Shriek Yelp Yelp Yelp

I winced. Whatever wolves were down there, they were in horrible pain. I couldn't imagine what Quint was doing to them, but I bet whatever it was, it was very, very bloody.

Remi clasped my arm gently. "If I'm not mistaken, that's Mateo with Lucien."

My eyes widened and butterflies fluttered in my chest. "I don't believe it."

Mateo's long black hair flickered his face and behind him. I couldn't tell if he was hurt or not.

Hades landed in the tower and I quickly moved my hands over him, examining his body for any wounds, but he was fine.

"He's a dragon," Raven said quietly. "His body may look like a lion's, but his soft scales are as tough as mine."

Lucien entered the tower and Mateo slipped from his back. My worst fears were realized. Bloody slashes and cuts and hideous bruises covered his body. He had iron cuffs on his wrists and ankles: he must have been chained up.

"Mateo." I knelt next to him. "You're hurt."

He lifted his head, his dark hair parting, revealing a puffy face and a black eye. "Salem?" His voice croaked. "Where am I?" He wobbled and sank to the ground in a faint.

"Mateo." I shook his shoulders, but only got a low moan.

"Salem, we have to get him inside before he freezes to death." Lucien knelt on the other side of Mateo.

I nodded. "Of course."

Grunting, he lifted Mateo's limp body and flung it over his broad shoulders. Damn, he was strong.

"Are you sure you can carry him?" I asked.

"Yes." But his answer was more of a groan.

We all followed Lucien down the dim stairwell. Mateo didn't move. Tears welled in my eyes as the flickering light reflected the lash marks on his sweaty body. Calvin really was a bastard. Who got off on inflicting torture like that?

Shuffle Shuffle Shuffle

Each time Lucien took a step I wrung my hands, wishing I could do something to help, but the passage was too narrow for anyone to walk alongside him. It was slow going down the stairwell, which seemed to go on for miles and miles. I wished Quint was here to help him carry Mateo, but the hunky vampire had disappeared. We were on our own. I glanced at the wall and the torches had melded our shadows into one, reminded me of a slow-moving tractor.

Suddenly, Lucien gasped loudly and wobbled for a split second as Mateo's body shifted on his shoulders. Pebbles tumbled down the stairs.

I grabbed one arm and Raven snagged the other.

"Thanks," he mumbled as we steadied him. Beads of sweat were dripping down his forehead and temples, making his hair stick to his face.

Please don't fall Please don't fall Please don't fall

I held my breath as he readjusted his footing. Somehow he managed to get down the steps without dropping Mateo.

When we reached the bottom of the stairs, the door swung open. Quint reached out and pulled Mateo off Lucien's shoulders.

Lucien panted angrily. "Where the hell have you been?"

Quint's green eyes turned dark red. "Making sure Calvin's spies never got back to their master." He held Mateo in his massive arms like he had Ashton and I saw blood all over them.

I shuddered, thinking of the mess he must have made, but it was probably for the best. I didn't want Calvin to know where we were.

A strange feeling came over me and I blurted, "Were they demon wolves?"

I wasn't sure why, but I didn't want them to be dead.

Quint shook his head. "No. They were Calvin's enforcers."

Lucien leaned against the wall, trying to catch his breath. "From what Hades and I saw, I think they were hunting Mateo down. I don't know how he escaped from Iredale Palace, but it mustn't have been easy."

Quint tilted his head. "I'll take this guy upstairs."

"I'll go with you." I wasn't going to leave Mateo for a second and no way was I going to use the *Book of Goody* again like I had on Ashton.

Hades followed me, as always.

Upstairs, Quint placed Mateo gently on a purple canopied king-sized bed that had a matching Cherrywood dresser and nightstand. The same color drapes hung at the windows all the way down to the floor. Anton sure liked these luxurious bedroom sets.

But right now, I didn't care about that. All that I cared about was Mateo. Every time I saw him, my feelings for him got stronger and stronger. There was something about him that drew me to him. "I need some rags and antiseptic to attend to his wounds."

Hades looked up at me with sad eyes as if he thought it was hopeless, and I almost burst into tears.

Don't cry Don't cry Don't cry

Quint opened another wooden door that I hadn't noticed. "This room has its own bathroom. You'll find everything you need in there including *Purifelio*, a potion from the Starlight Kingdom that will help heal his wounds."

"Thank you." I tried to force a smile, but it was difficult.

"You're welcome." He bowed slightly. "Call me if you need anything."

I cleared my throat. "I will." I glanced at Mateo's wrists. "Wait—"

"Yes?" Quint asked.

"Can you get those manacles off his wrists and ankles?"

"Of course. I'll be right back."

He left, and I was alone with Mateo. I brushed Mateo's hair from his feverish face. "What did Calvin do to you?" I murmured.

He didn't answer, but at least he was breathing, unlike poor Ashton. I bit back a sob. I couldn't think about Ashton right now. I had to focus on Mateo.

Hades hopped onto the bed, curled up next to him, and sighed miserably. I had a sudden idea.

"Can you heal him, Hades?"

Hades got up and opened his mouth. He inhaled but nothing

happened. No dark sludge came out of Mateo and I couldn't help but wonder if it had something to do with those damn manacles.

The little Catalan dragon hung his head dejectedly and whimpered. I rubbed his mane. "Thanks for trying, buddy. It's not your fault—it's Calvin's magic."

Hades raised his head and licked my hand.

"Stay with Mateo. I'll be right back," I whispered.

I rushed into the bathroom and wet a washcloth. Under the white marble sink, I found some bandages, and just like Quint had said, there was no antiseptic. Instead I found a glass bottle filled with a pink liquid marked *Purifelio* and hoped it would heal those ugly lashes all over Mateo's body.

The only thing I could think about was Hayley. What if she had been forced to use dark magic on him? I was pretty sure that the potion wouldn't work then.

But I had to try.

Just as I pulled up a leather chair next to Mateo's bed, Quint came into the room with a bolt cutter.

"Will those work?"

"As long as the manacles are not enchanted," he said.

I slumped down in the leather chair. "Oh, God. Seriously?"

His face turned grim. "Seriously. Calvin likes his dark magic." He put the bolt cutters to the metal, but as soon as he did, black sparks flew out and sent him and the bolt cutters careening backward. He smashed into the wall, leaving an imprint, and slid down onto his ass.

I rushed over to him. "Quint, are you okay?"

"Yeah, I'm fine," he snapped angrily. He shook his head as if trying to clear it. "Whatever spell that witch used, it's a doozy. I'm afraid your friend won't fare well. I'm sorry."

My gut tightened at his words.

He stumbled to his feet. I reached to grip his arm to steady him, but he jerked away.

"I don't need any help," he said gruffly.

"Fine." I dropped my arms to my side. Definitely an old grump. Damned handsome, but also damned grumpy.

He grabbed the bolt cutters and gave me a slight frown as he headed for the door. "Call me if you need anything."

"I will." But what could he do? Or anyone? I felt sick to think that Mateo might suffer the same fate as Ashton.

I hurried back to Mateo who still hadn't made a sound. I opened the jar of *Purifelio* that I had left on the nightstand, and found it to be fragrant, like a eucalyptus candle. Just the scent reduced the tension in my muscles. I hoped it would help Mateo, too.

I poured some of the pink liquid on the damp washcloth and then wiped Mateo's sweaty, bruised face. He took a quivering breath. Maybe it was helping a little. I gently wiped down the deep, ugly lashes on his chiseled body, trying not to cry when he hissed in pain. I wasn't sure if the *Purifelio* was stinging him or if the dark magic was rejecting the healing potion.

God, I wished Anton or Dr. Greenwood was here. They would know what to do.

Remi burst into the bedroom. "Salem, come quick." Her voice shook with excitement.

I twisted the washcloth, squeezing out the pink stained water into a bowl. "I can't, Remi. I have to take care of Mateo."

"No, you don't understand. It's Ashton."

I stiffened and then glanced over my shoulder. "What about him?"

"He's alive."

9

I just stared at Remi who stood in the doorway. Had she lost her mind? Why was she tugging at my heartstrings like that?

"What are you talking about?" I asked dully as I returned to wiping down Mateo's body.

"Salem, please. Just come." She motioned with her arm excitedly. "Come on. Come and see for yourself." Her voice reminded me of a teenager screaming on a rollercoaster.

I hesitated, not sure I should leave Mateo. What if he awoke and I wasn't here?

"Salem, please. Ashton's asking for you."

I blinked. "He is?"

She gently touched my back. "I'll stay with Mateo. Go see for yourself."

The Catalan dragon got up as if to follow me, but I shook my head. "No, Hades. Stay with Mateo."

He plopped back down and sighed heavily.

"Thanks, buddy." I ran my hand down his back. I still couldn't believe what Remi was saying.

Raven and Lucien were waiting for me in the hallway, beaming.

"This way, girl. Come on." Raven looped her arm through mine and tilted her head toward another bedroom. She led me into the room and my mouth dropped open. Ashton was leaning against the headboard. His hair was tousled and he still looked pale, but he was very much alive.

Confusion glistened in his eyes. "Salem?"

"Oh, Ashton." I ran over to him and sat on the edge of the bed. I took his clammy hand in mine. "I can't believe it."

He gave me a weary grin. "Me either." He wiped the beads of sweat off his face with his arm. "It was so weird. I slipped into darkness and despair. Desolation. I was lost and couldn't find my out but then there was a bright light, leading me out." His tired voice was like music to my ears.

I blinked away the tears threatening to fall. "Really?"

"Yeah. I swear it was your voice."

"My voice?" I put my hand on my chest. "How can this be? You've been out…I mean you were dead…this whole day."

His eyes widened. "I was?"

I nodded. "Yes. You were." I still had trouble believing my own eyes that he had come back to us.

"Remi told me that you used the *Book of Goody* to heal me."

I lowered my head. "I tried. It didn't do any good."

He squeezed my hand gently. "Salem, what are you talking about? I'm alive because you used that spell book."

I looked up at him. "Ashton, I didn't even know what I was doing. I'm not sure if any of this is even real."

"Please," he snorted. "You're not just a wolf. You're powerful, Salem. You have the power of the first Moon king in you."

My brows furrowed. "You make it sound like only my ancestors possess this magical power."

"Because that's the truth. None of the other first kings in the other wolf kingdoms possessed any magic."

The image of the first king popped into my mind. "I never knew that," I said softly. "Why don't the others?"

"Because they're all pure bloods."

I cringed. "So I'm the biggest freak in the forest?" This was foster care all over again. I was the new kid that everyone pretended didn't exist.

He shrugged. "They don't understand. These days, wolves and witches don't exactly trust each other. There was a time when they did, and the witches created the portals for the wolves to travel to the different kingdoms, but then the witches' High Priestess aligned herself with the Unseelie during a supernatural war and all previous allegiances were forgotten."

I didn't want to think about the wolf kingdoms and their politics and prejudices. That was the least of my troubles right now. "Did Raven and the others tell you that Mateo's here too?"

He frowned. "No. Is he all right?"

I cleared my throat, refusing to give in to the sob that was bubbling upside me. "No, he's not." I didn't cry, but my voice suddenly turned into a bullfrog.

Dread filled his tired eyes. "What happened?"

I threaded my fingers distractedly through my tangled hair. "Same as you. Tortured. Barely alive. Plus, he's got these stupid manacles on his wrists and ankles that not even Quint could remove."

"What do you mean?" He lowered his voice, as if he were afraid someone could be listening.

I told him what happened.

"Shit." He squeezed my hand. "Salem, you have to use the *Book of Goody* to save him."

"No." I wiggled my hand free and crossed my arms. "I'm no good at it. I could kill him."

"You don't understand. Those manacles are cursed. They're draining the life force out of him. He'll die soon if you don't do anything."

I could feel the blood drain from my face. "Oh, God."

"Hurry."

"But Ashton—"

"Do you want him to die?"

Fear fluttered in my chest, crushing my lungs and speeding up my heartbeat. Goosebumps broke out all over me. "No. Of course not. But Hades or Raven—"

"They can't help. Raven can drain supernatural powers, and Hades can suck out Unseelie or Dark Demon magic, but this is neither. Witch magic is different. Their abilities won't do anything."

"But I'm not even a witch. I'm a wolf."

He gave me an impish smile. "Now, you're thinking like I did, feeling like I felt. You're afraid, Salem. You're afraid of who you are. Don't be. You have to embrace it if you ever hope to defeat Calvin."

I looked at him curiously. "You've changed."

His green eyes darkened to an angry gold. "Being tortured can do that." But then the shadow left his face. "But I wasn't alone. Hayley was with me and she's the one that really opened my eyes." He cupped my chin with his long fingers. "Go and save Mateo, Salem. Trust in yourself."

I hesitated and bit my lip.

"Go," he urged.

I reluctantly got up and headed downstairs to get the *Book of Goody*. It was still where I left it on the coffee table. Raven and Lucien were drinking coffee in the living room.

Raven frowned. "What are you doing?"

I picked up the book and immediately those strange sensations moved through me again.

"Ashton says if I don't get those manacles off Mateo, he'll die. They're cursed and draining the life force from him."

Raven got up from the sofa and gave me a hug. "You can do this, Salem. You healed Ashton. Sure, it took a while, but sometimes spells don't work right away. Trust in yourself."

Everyone kept saying that, but I wasn't sure I was buying it.

As we all went upstairs, I clutched the thick leather book to my chest tightly. I really had no idea whether this would work or not, and I had a gut feeling this would be harder than it was with Ashton because of the damn manacles.

My uncle was a serious douche bag with a capital D!

We walked into the bedroom. Remi was sitting on Mateo's bed, holding his hand. She looked up with tears glistening in her eyes. "His breath is getting shallower and shallower."

My heart twisted in despair. I couldn't lose him, I just couldn't. "Yes," I said glumly. "It's the manacles, they're cursed. Quint tried cutting them off and he was thrown across the room."

She looked at the punched-out drywall. "So, that's what happened to the wall. I was wondering. The dark magic must be really strong."

"Super strong," I muttered. I looked at each of them, even Hades. "When I do this, I don't think any of you should be in the room."

"No chance, sweet pea." Raven elbowed me gently in the ribs. "We're a team. For better or worse."

I looked at Lucien who only gave me a wry smile and shrugged. "Hey, she's the boss. Whatever she says."

Hades lifted his head and clenched the quilt between his paws as if to say, 'I'm not going anywhere, either'.

Remi gave me a long, hard stare. "We're in this together, Salem."

Quint walked into the room and folded his arms. "I'm in, too. Someone's got to clean up the mess."

Then he put his hand on his sword and poked his head out the doorway. "You idiot. Get your ass back in bed."

Seriously, Ashton?

"No." Ashton fell into Quinton, who put his arm over his shoulder and practically carried him into Mateo's bedroom.

Ashton panted. "I'm...part...of this team...too."

"That's it!" Lucien said. "We'll call ourselves the Vindicators."

I frowned. "Why vindicators?"

Remi narrowed her eyes. "Because it's time for you to take back your crown. And for us to set our people free, and avenge my sister's and her husband's death."

I looked at each of them. "The Vindicators it is, then." I stared down at Mateo. "Let's leave no fallen man behind." Especially the man that bunched my panties.

The *Book of Goody* trembled in my arms and its power slid over me like a roaring wave.

T hat same voice whispered in my mind.

We can heal him. Put your hand on me.

Just as I did with Ashton, I spread my fingers and palm over the book. "Show me."

Tingling sensations whirled within me and pink swirls glided around my fingers. Wind swooshed around me, sending chills down my back. I opened the book as if in a trance.

I flipped through the pages, stopping sooner than I had last time. This time I was just a few pages into the book and the words of the top of the page were *Vengeiatis Infectundo*. The introduction to the spell said it was used to break a curse on objects, but warned if a person was wearing the cursed object, they would have to be restrained because a battle between good and evil would begin. The cursed object would inflict pain and would try to kill the host unless it was removed.

"This is bad," I said. "Mateo could die if I use this spell. I fucking hate this."

"He's going to die anyway if you don't," Quint said bluntly. I gritted my teeth.

"Okay. Unlike Ashton, this is going to hurt him," I said. "Lucien and Quint, you're going to have to hold him down."

Hades growled.

"Yes, you too, buddy."

Hades crawled onto Mateo's legs, pinning him to the bed. Remi got out of the way and she and Raven held hands. Quint lowered Ashton into the leather chair next to the canopy bed, then he and Lucien pushed down on Mateo's arms.

I took a deep breath and looked at them. "Are we ready?"

"Do it," Quint said. "Quick. This guy's cold as ice."

In a loud, clear voice, I said, *"Vengeiatis Infectundo."*

Pink sparkles swirled out of the *Book of Goody* and landed on Mateo.

Aaargh

He screamed and arched his back. Lucien and Quint fought to hold his arms to the bed. He kicked his legs and Hades had to use his entire body weight to keep from being thrown off. Black stars circled Mateo's wrists faster and faster. Blood seeped from the manacles.

"You can't stop, Salem," Ashton said softly. "You have to keep going. His life depends on it."

Tears streaming down my face, I yelled again. *"Vengeiatis Infectundo."*

Mateo let out another blood-curdling scream, shattering my heart into a million pieces.

10

*M*ateo thrashed his head from side to side on the bed and blood dripped down his lips.

"I can't do this," I muttered through clenched teeth.

Raven grabbed my shoulders and shook me. "Yes, you can. If you stop now, the dark magic will take him."

I nodded. She stepped away.

This time I held out my hand. "Vengeiatis Infectundo." Pulsing sensations moved through me and pink stars jetted from of my fingers, attacking the black ones encircling Mateo's wrists and ankles.

He went into convulsions, bouncing up and down on the bed as if he were possessed, frothing at the mouth.

"Dammit. Hold onto him," Quint yelled as his muscles strained holding Mateo's arm.

"I'm trying. But it's like he's turned into the Incredible Hulk."

"Say it again," Ashton beseeched me. "Now."

God, this had to stop. I squeezed my eyes shut.

Please, help him

Power snaked through me, ten times greater than before, and I arched my back and spread my arms out wide. I looked up and saw Remi gaping at me.

"Oh, my." She covered her mouth with her palm.

I felt something moving within me, like it had taken over.

"Vengeiatis Infectundo." The voice that came from my mouth didn't sound like mine.

More and more power surged through me like an angry flood until it finally reached a fever pitch. I aimed my fingers at Mateo and more pink streams whirled around the black stars, shooting arrows at them. One by one, the black stars exploded.

Click

Click

Click

Click

The manacles fell off Mateo's wrists and ankles. His convulsions slowly ceased.

The power within me dissipated like morning dew at dawn. I couldn't stop trembling. Beads of sweat dripped down face and my hair stuck to my damp cheeks. My shoulders slumped weakly and my arms dangled at my side. I felt as limp as a crushed blade of wet grass. Everyone was looking at me strangely, as if they were waiting for something else to happen.

Frowning, Remi wiped Mateo's sweaty face with a cloth. "He's breathing, but it's still very weak." She put her hand over his heart. "And his heartbeat is very, very faint. I'm not sure he's out of the woods just yet."

"Salem," Ashton said softly. "The manacles trapping the magic inside him are off, but you still need to heal him."

I leaned against the wall, still catching my breath. "What are you talking about, Ashton?"

"He's still cursed, same as me." Ashton met my gaze. "Whatever spell you used to heal me, you need to use on Mateo."

"I'm not sure he would even survive the spell." I dragged my fingers through my hair.

Remi looked up. "You have to try. If you don't, he probably won't last the night."

Every excuse was on the tip of my tongue, but the desperate gazes of my friends busted all of them. I was beaten. I had no choice but to try.

My hands trembling, I picked up the book.

Help me, please

All of my strength had been drained, but that same invisible force moved my fingers through the pages until I reached the Illumiicus Honorulus, the same spell I had used on Ashton. God, I didn't know if I was strong enough to muster enough magic to help him.

You are, the same voice echoed in my mind.

Calling on all my determination, I took a deep breath and held out my trembling hand. "Illumiicus Honorulus."

Pink streams flew out of my fingertips, then turned into little stars that hovered over Mateo's still body. The stars slowly settled into his body. More and more streams jetted out of my fingers and I could fell the energy leaving me like the air out of a burst balloon. My vision blurred, and brown, pink, and white dots floated in front of me. My head fell back and my eyes fluttered shut. My knees buckled.

"Salem," someone yelled.

Strong arms caught me and I remembered nothing more.

I woke to the smell of lavender and warmth on my cheeks. I opened my eyes to see a red canopy bed and sunlight streaming in through the window. I looked down and saw Hades curled up on my legs, looking up at me with his golden eyes like a big puppy dog and thumping his tail.

Someone with brownish-blonde tousled hair was asleep in the chair next to me, softly snoring, and I realized it was Ashton.

"Ashton, she's finally awake," a masculine voice said.

I turned my head and my heart quickened and leapt for joy to find myself staring into Mateo's dark brown eyes. His curly hair stuck out everywhere and dark circles were under his bloodshot eyes. If I didn't know better, I would think he was suffering from a hangover.

But he was alive. He was alive.

Tears pushed on the back of my eyelids. "Mateo," I croaked. My mouth and throat were so dry it was the only word I could manage.

He shook his head and took my hand. "Damn, girl."

I was surprised that his own hand was shaking. Was there still some dark magic inside him?

Hades nudged my other hand and I gave him a loving smile as I petted his thick mane. He purred beneath my palm.

"You look like you could use some water."

Someone lifted my shoulders gently off my pillow and I looked up at Ashton, who looked just has disheveled as Mateo.

"Here, drink." He lifted a glass of water to my parched lips.

I drank greedily, the cool water gushing down my throat and running down my chin.

"Easy, woman." He took the cup away.

I licked my lips. "More," I croaked again.

Ashton sighed but returned the cup to my lips so I could down the rest of the water.

Concern filled his green eyes. "How are you feeling?"

I inhaled and exhaled several times before I answered him. "Like I've been in the desert for weeks."

"It's the magic," Ashton said. "It completely drained you." His voice was unsteady, as if he was struggling to stay in control.

His words were terrifying. God, could using magic kill me?

He gently lowered me back onto the pillow and I looked at both of them. Their faces were so grim there was something definitely wrong.

I moistened my lips and cleared my throat several times. "How long have I been here?"

"You've been in a coma for almost ten days," Mateo said gravely. "We didn't know..." His voice trailed off and he lowered his head, then returned his gaze to me. "We didn't know if you were going to make it."

"Ah, so she's awake." A woman wearing a crown of white roses upon her brow entered the room. Her white gown shimmered around her.

She gave me a warm smile. "I'm the Fae Queen Gwendoline of the Starlight Kingdom. Anton sent for me."

My eyes widened. "He did? Why?"

Her smile turned weary. "Isn't obvious? You were dying, Salem. You did not yet have enough magic inside you to cast three powerful spells in a row." Her brows furrowed. "Surely Anton told you this?"

My cheeks burned. "He did, but I couldn't...I couldn't let my friends die."

"You shouldn't have used the last spell on me," Mateo grumbled.

I glared. "Would you rather be dead?"

He clamped his jaw tight and narrowed his tired eyes, but he didn't answer me. The truth was, I would have done anything to save him.

"Don't be too harsh on her, Mateo," Queen Gwendoline said. "I believe her self-sacrifice is why the magic allowed me to save her."

She talked as if the magic was capable of thought. "It can decide that?"

"Yes. Tell me, when you have used the Book of Goody, have you heard a voice?"

My jaw dropped. "How did you know? I thought I was going crazy."

"No, that is the magic." She strolled over to my bed. "Think of it as a second part of you. The book taps into the part of you that is magical."

The queen placed her palm on my forehead and a sense of calm flushed through me. I could breathe easier and the dryness in my throat seemed to ease. She looked down at me. "Feel better?"

I nodded. "Yeah, I do. Thank you."

"I have the gift of healing. It dwells inside me, like your magic resides in you. You're very powerful, Salem. Much like your ancestor, the first King, and this is why your uncle is so afraid of you."

I winced. "So people keep telling me."

"If they keep telling you that, doesn't that mean it's true?" She looked between Mateo and Ashton. "Have you told her yet?"

Mateo let out a frustrated sigh and the lines around his eyes tensed.

Ashton gritted his teeth. "Seriously? She just woke up from a fucking coma."

I gave them each a sharp look. "What? What aren't you telling me?"

"There's nothing you can do about it." Mateo leaned his head back on the chair. "So, we didn't want you to worry."

I turned to Ashton, but he was staring out the window.

Cowards. Both of them.

Queen Gwendoline cocked her eyebrow at my two-would-be heroes. "Well, I guess I'm the one to tell you."

I met her gaze. "Tell me what?"

Queen Gwendoline tilted her head. "Your friend, Mateo, had help escaping from Iredale Palace."

I frowned. "From whom?"

"King Calvin's daughter, Gloria."

"I left the Royal Guard." Mateo scrubbed his face. "I'm an outcast, slated for death, and still she risked her life to save me."

"We owe her one, then."

"I'm afraid it's not that simple." Queen Gwendoline's face had turned grave. "The royal guard caught Gloria and rumor has it she's scheduled for execution."

"What?!" I couldn't believe it. "How can he do that? She's his only child."

Sadness flared in the queen's eyes. "Calvin looks at his children and even his wife as assets. He's more like the old human kings who viewed their wives and children, especially daughters, as chattel."

Ashton got up and looked at the window. "We can't let her die. She saved me and Mateo" ...he lowered his head... "and now, she's paying with her life." There was something else in his voice. It sounded like his heart was breaking.

I stared at his drooping shoulders and then it hit me like a bucket of ice water. "Ashton," I said softly. "Is Gloria your mate?"

He put his palms on the glass window. "I've fought it for so long. She's Calvin's daughter. I didn't want it to be her." He turned and held my gaze. "I wanted it to be you. But..." His voice trailed off as if he was struggling to rein in those feelings.

I sat straighter. "We won't let her die."

Mateo folded his arms. "Do you think you can get to her? Calvin will have Iredale Palace locked down tighter than Fort Knox."

"I'm sure that's true," Queen Gwendoline said. "If we use conventional methods."

Mateo's scowl grew even deeper. "Meaning?"

She looked at me. "Salem's power is growing."

"Not the Book of Goody again," Mateo said angrily. He gestured with his arm. "That thing almost killed her."

Ashton turned around. Tears glistened in his eyes. "I can't let Gloria die. I know she's spoiled, and Calvin's daughter, but I can't...I just can't...I'll go myself if I have to..." His voice trailed off.

I looked at Mateo. "You won't have to."

He threw up his arms. "This is ridiculous." He dragged his

fingers through his hair. "There's no way we will come out of there alive. Did any of you consider that this may be a trap?"

Ashton briefly glanced up at the ceiling and sighed. "It might be."

I sighed heavily. "My uncle may be a lot of things, but he's not stupid."

"He could be torturing her," Ashton continued miserably. "Just like he did Mateo and me."

My gut sickened at the thought. "Would he really do that to his daughter?"

Queen Gwendoline's eyes filled with sorrow. "I wish I could say otherwise, but alas, it's true. Anyone who thwarts his path is severely punished—and as in poor Gloria's case—executed."

he tension in the room escalated as each of us became lost in our own thoughts. Weariness still gripped me tightly but I felt stronger. The sunlight warmed my cheeks, thawing the cold and despair that had kept me in its clutches.

I stroked Hades' silky mane. "So when do we leave?"

Mateo chuckled and shook his head. "We? Are you serious?" His sarcastic tone pricked my pride.

I narrowed my eyes and gritted my teeth. "I'm dead serious. I'm not staying behind, Mateo. This is my fight."

He clasped my hand and squeezed it gently. "But Salem, you're not strong enough. Not yet." His husky voice tamed the anger that had been brewing inside me.

I stared into his eyes that were filled with concern, but also a glint of something else, something that stirred not only me, but my wolf. "Do you want Gloria to die?"

He lowered his head. "You know I don't, but I can't risk lose you. You're our only hope." His voice was as soft and tender as his kisses.

I didn't answer him. He was so damn handsome that for a

minute I couldn't think and was lost on where we were, just like in the tunnel, but then something occurred to me.

"Mateo, you're being hunted—"

"We all are," Ashton said grimly. "If I'm not mistaken, I bet Calvin's next move will be to send Velkan and the demon wolves to track us down."

"Yes, and they'll track us here," Mateo said. "It's just a matter of time."

"Maybe. Maybe not." My voice drew all their eyes to me.

Mateo frowned. "What do you mean?" Wariness was etched on his handsome face and clung to his words.

I looked between Mateo and Ashton. "If we head back to the palace, we'll lure them away from Anton's cabin. The others will be safe then."

Remi walked into the room, scowling, with Quint right behind her. "You think you can tuck me away like a china doll on a high shelf? Don't even think it."

Quint held my gaze. "I thought we were a team. Or was that all a lie?"

I winced as if he had slapped me. "No. I just don't—"

Remi sat on the edge of my bed and patted my leg. "I know, honey. You don't want any of us to get hurt. But we can't let that poor girl die." She glanced over at Mateo. "And yes, I know we could be walking into a trap. But what choice do we have? Gloria's life is in danger."

I leaned my head back on my headboard. "Great. Calvin has us right where he wants us."

"You forget about the *Book of Goody*," Queen Gwendoline said. "Right now, it's your biggest weapon and it will eventually unleash a power in you that will help you defeat your uncle and restore happiness and peace to your kingdom."

Fear chipped away at my determination, sending chills down my spine, and I shivered.

She cocked her eyebrow. "Or are you not up to the challenge?"

"You're forgetting about Hayley. Calvin will force her to thwart us at every turn." Mateo's grim warning turned my blood into ice.

"This is true." Queen Gwendoline nodded. "Calvin knows Salem possesses magic like the first King, but we have an advantage. He doesn't know we have the *Book of Goody*. Salem, you must use this advantage against him and fight his witch with your own magic."

My eyes widened. "But she's powerful."

Queen Gwendoline smiled. "So are you."

Something in her voice awoke something inside me. Power and confidence surged through me, chasing away the weariness. My wolf was coming.

"Before she does anything," Remi said, "she needs to eat. Quint has prepared a delicious breakfast downstairs. Can you get up, or do you want me to bring you a tray?"

My stomach grumbled and Hades thumped his tail on the bed. I gave them both a small smile. "Well, if I'm going to fight the demon wolves and a witch, I guess I'd better get out of bed."

I just hoped I could.

Hades licked my hand.

Mateo flicked his gaze over me. "Are you sure you're strong enough?"

Hades growled softly, but Mateo ignored him.

I tilted my chin up in defiance. "Of course." Except I quivered underneath his perceptive gaze.

Mateo sat back in his chair. "Okay then, get up."

God, he just wouldn't give up his position that I wasn't strong enough. No one countered him, as if they were holding their collective breath to see if I really was going to be able to take on the demon wolves and Hayley.

Hades hopped off the bed and eagerly looked at me, clearly wanting me to follow him. I took a deep cleansing breath. My body trembled, and then like a bolt of lightning my wolf came forth, tearing through my clothes. Their eyes widened as I shifted into my beautiful white wolf and I hopped off the bed. Renewed confidence and strength pumped through me, and I felt like I could take on the world. It was as if my wolf knew I wasn't strong enough but she was—strong enough to tear my uncle to pieces.

I joined Hades and looked around the room, daring anyone to challenge me.

Mateo broke out in a smile. "I guess you showed me."

A sudden craving coursed through me. My wolf needed to run. She'd been cooped so long inside my body and needed freedom. Somehow, I knew that would bring me strength.

Without waiting for anyone else, I bolted out of the bedroom with Hades right behind me.

"Salem, wait." Mateo and Ashton called out together.

But I didn't stop. I needed freedom—to feel the wind on my face, to stretch my legs.

I clawed at the oak door, needing to get out. My wolf was determined and desperate.

Thundering footsteps raced down the stairs.

Mateo reached for me. "Salem, no." I snarled, the hair on my back bristling, daring him to come any closer.

He didn't understand. They needed to follow me. We needed to become a pack if we were going to defeat Calvin, Velkan, and the demon wolves. I couldn't do it alone.

I needed them with me.

Queen Gwendoline's gaze swept over all their concerned faces. "I think your future queen has given you clear orders. She needs to run free and wants you to run with her. Or are you disobeying her first command?"

They all looked at each other, startled, but then Mateo broke out into a grin.

He looked at each of them in turn. "The queen has spoken. Let's all go for a run."

Faster than I thought possible, my team stripped, except for

Quint, and shifted into their wolves. Each was a different color—Remi red, Ashton gray, and Mateo black. I was the largest.

Quint lowered the drawbridge and we all bolted out into the forest, including Hades, who flew above the castle, and Quint, who was determined not to be left behind and changed into a large black bat so he could soar into the air and fly with Hades.

Cold wind rushed over me as my paws barely touched the frozen forest floor. I ran as fast as I could, taking in the cool mountain air, filling my lungs with energy. Adrenaline exploded inside me. For the first time, we ran as a pack—a crazy pack that included a Catalan dragon and a vampire. I detected the scent of deer and elk and sensed their fear, but we weren't hunting them. There was something else we wanted to hunt more.

We jumped over tree logs, crashed through frozen streams, and thundered over the snow as I led the pack up a random trail. I wasn't sure where it would take us, but I needed to see over the mountain tops and the trees and look toward Iredale Palace. The trail ended at large cliff that overlooked a roaring river below us. I stopped and sat, my team fanning out behind me.

Wind gushed over us but my fur kept me warm. Sniffing, I could scent Iredale Palace. It was located behind the second mountain peak.

So. The showdown was coming. I needed to be ready for it.

I turned to face my pack. Whether I wanted to be or not, I was their leader and I wouldn't let them down. Once again, I had led them on a merry chase straight into danger, but this time we were a team.

My wolf pushed inside me, uncovering a feeling that had been long buried. Tingling sensations rolled over me and I gave in to the power.

Mateo's eyes darkened as if he sensed what was happening with me, and something glinted behind his perceptive gaze. My wolf nudged me and a single word burst into my brain.

Mine...

Aaaaaaoooo

I howled. My wolves joined the call.

Aaaaaaoo

Hades roared, accompanying us.

Shriek Shriek Shriek

Quint's bat was the castrato in our choir's song. But it wasn't a song. It was a challenge, a battle cry to Calvin that we were coming.

In the distance, my ears picked up another symphony.

Aaaaaaooo Aaaaaoo Aaaaaooooo

Chills crept down my spine and I shivered, shaking my fur. My heart quickened, sending blood pumping through me faster and faster. It was an answer to our challenge. The demon wolves had heard and accepted it. We would meet on the battlefield sooner rather than later.

My wolf's excitement made me quiver as Mateo stepped forward. His wolf was only slighter smaller than mine, but he had a commanding presence that couldn't be denied. It was easy to imagine him as the leader of the Royal Guard and picture him facing down Calvin alone in times gone by. He stepped forward and nuzzled my cheek, sending waves of comfort through me, coupled with a desire I never knew existed and feelings I had never felt for any other guy. It was overwhelming how much I wanted him.

Ashton came over next, but Mateo snarled as if to say I was his. Ashton lowered his head and whimpered. I licked Mateo's muzzle and he stepped aside allowing Ashton to approach me, but I could sense something had changed between us.

Next, Hades buried his head in my chest. Remi laid next to Hades, resting one of her paws on mine. Quint stepped forward and the massive bat spread his wings around us. We were together.

We were a team.

We were the Vindicators.

We huddled together on the cold mountaintop for several long minutes. The demon wolves howled in the distance and it sounded like they were getting closer.

Something stirred inside me.

Something I didn't think was possible.

Something was missing.

The demon wolves.

They were part of my pack.

And I needed to claim them as mine.

You know how to find them. I can help you, a voice whispered in my mind.

I recognized that low voice. I had heard it when I had cast those spells. Somehow the magic from the *Book of Goody* had followed me here, or maybe since I had used the book, I had unleashed it and now the magic was always going to be with me.

One thing I knew for sure, the answer was in the *Book of Goody.*

All I had to do was find the right spell and hope it didn't kill me.

12

I turned to look at Mateo and the rest of the Vindicators and then I burst out at a dead run back to Anton's cabin, my paws nearly flying over the wintry terrain, leaping over rocks and tree branches, and pulling on speed as I neared the house. Desire surged through me and a hunger pushed through me, not for food, but for physical touch.

Yes, I needed to claim the demon wolves as part of my pack, but even more importantly I needed to claim Mateo as my mate. Now. I was almost weak with need.

Mateo ran by my side and I wondered if he felt the same pounding urge that I did as we neared Anton's cabin.

Queen Gwendoline stood in the doorway, waiting for us. Mateo and I leapt past her, not stopping, and headed straight upstairs. We raced up the stairs two, three at time and leapt into my bedroom. Mateo shifted first and slammed the door shut behind us. God, he was magnificent with his bulging muscles, defined lines that contoured his body. His long dark hair flared over his massive shoulders.

Mine.

The word echoed in my mind again and again.

"Shift," he said in a husky voice.

Without hesitation, I did as he asked. My gaze flicked down his chest and took in the flat stomach and the v lines that led down to his huge cock, which was fully erect. Oh, my God. My heart and lungs stopped.

Heat swept over my body and I covered myself with my hands, trying to shield myself from the passion in his eyes. The room turned colder, making my nipples bud and giving me a rash of goosebumps everywhere. Or was it really cold? Something had suddenly made me into a shy wallflower.

He cocked his eyebrow as he approached. "What are you doing?"

I looked down at my wiggling toes. "I'm...I'm just nervous, I guess."

He gave me a smile that warmed my insides. "I can see that." He clasped my chin with his rough fingers, forcing me to look into his deep dark eyes. "Don't be. You never have to hide yourself from me. You're beautiful. And you're mine."

"Mateo," I murmured. It was the only thing I could to think to say.

He moved his hand slowly, cupping my cheek, to brush a wandering stray hair behind my ear, then threaded his fingers through my tangled waves. "Are you a virgin, Salem?"

I licked my trembling lips. "Yes." My voice was soft, but my heart was thumping harder and harder.

"So, I'll be your one and only." Possessiveness echoed in his voice.

I nodded wordlessly.

I could feel the tremor in his hands as they slipped down my neck, then my shoulders, and for two agonizing seconds I thought he would stop, but he didn't. He parted his lips, a harsh groan of abandoned desire escaping from them, and then his arms went around my waist, pulling me against his hard chest, squashing my breasts. I could feel his heart beating as fast as mine, and he drove the air from my lungs as I gasped and his lips captured mine. He devoured me, the passionate kiss of a man who was as desperate to claim me as I was to claim him.

I wrapped my arms around his shoulders and returned his kiss with abandon. I trembled, sending an earthquake of rumbling tremors down my body, turning my blood steamy hot. Pure, raw lust eclipsed my fear and I dug my fingers into his thick hair, refusing to let him break away, not even to take a breath.

His mouth stay fastened over mine as his hands moved down my curves, sending tingling sensations through me. I arched my head back, whimpering when I felt his lips around my nipple, tugging and sucking. The stubble of his beard chafed my skin, making me even hotter. My legs shook and he lifted me into his arms, carrying me to the bed, his hot mouth never leaving my breast. He laid me gently onto the bed and climbed on top of me. Crying out his name, I melted forward, my fingers twisting into his hair, and he obliged me by sucking harder, laving my flesh with his tongue as I made small, smothered cries.

He slipped his hand down my tummy until he reached my secret red curls and then gently stroked my inner folds, stirring rivers of sensations within my inner core.

"You're driving me mad," I murmured.

"Oh, I've only just begun, princess."

He left my breast and kissed and licked his way down my stomach until he reached my belly button and his tongue swirled around and around while his hand stroked me. I thrashed my head back and forth on the bed and my fingers bunched the quilt, hanging on for dear life as stars danced in front of my vision and my nipples budded.

His other hand pushed open my trembling thighs. Before I could take another breath, he left my bellybutton and pushed his masterful tongue inside my feathery curls, licking and lapping at me. I had to dig my fingers deeper into the quilt to keep from launching myself off the bed.

"You have to stop..." I panted. "I don't think I can survive this. It feels too good."

"You will. You must." His desperate voice matched the need growing inside me that only he could satisfy.

"Then don't make me wait. Take me. Please." I scrubbed his hair with my fingers and dug my nails into his broad shoulders.

He looked up and gave me a devilish grin. "Your wish is my command, your majesty." He slowly climbed up me, his long hair teasing my hot skin. "Spread your beautiful legs for your mate."

I widened my quaking thighs and he nestled his hips between them. I immediately tensed. His cock pushed against my inner thigh and I shuddered, not sure I could accommodate his large size.

Sweet concern filled his eyes. "Are you nervous, princess?" He lowered his head. "Or do you not want to do this since I'm only a guard?" His eyes darkened. "Not even a guard anymore."

I cupped his rugged cheek. "Mateo, I grew up in foster care. I'm not royalty."

He kissed the tip of my nose. "Yes, you are, whether you want to admit it or not."

I thought occurred to me and I stilled. "Wait. Is the only reason you want to be with me" ...I bit my lip... "that I'm the missing princess?"

He frowned and arched his back, putting his weight on his arms. "How can you say that? Do you remember when I found in your trailer?"

"Yes," I stretched out the word warily. "Why?"

He took several deep breaths before he answered. "The first time I caught your scent, I knew."

"You knew what?"

"That you were mine. That you were my mate. But I didn't know if you would accept me." He ran his finger down my collarbone, making me shiver. "There's such a thing as rejected mates."

I gave him a teasing smile and twirled my finger in a lock of his hair. "You thought I would reject you?"

He shrugged and didn't answer. Uneasiness flared in his eyes, as if he was still afraid I'd confirm his worst fear.

My heart bled for him. I knew that feeling of guarding yourself to keep people from hurting you. It was the way I had survived growing up in foster care. "Mateo, I don't know anything about this mate thing, but you stole my heart the moment I saw you sitting on my couch." I put my finger on his frowning lips. "Even though you did break into my trailer."

He nipped at my finger playfully. "You forget, I saved your life that day."

My smile faded and my overwhelming feelings for him swelled in my chest, pushing my heart and lungs against my ribs. "I've never forgotten anything you've done for me." I couldn't get the three little words out that I wanted to say to him. They would strip away my last wall, making me vulnerable. I wasn't ready for that.

He searched my eyes and then he kissed me hard and I slid my fingers up and down his back, marveling at the muscles, moving underneath my palms.

His hard cock pushed against my thigh and I tensed, thinking about how badly this was going to hurt.

He stopped kissing me. "What's wrong?"

Heat spread across my cheeks. "I just don't know if you'll fit. You're huge."

"Do you trust me?" He stroked the curls between my legs again, replacing the tension with renewed need.

Biting my lips, I nodded. Why shouldn't I? Trust never came easy for me, but since I'd met him, he'd done everything he could do to protect me.

He planted kisses on my throat, the stubble of beard scratching me, his mustache tickling me. I slowly relaxed and then he removed his hand and arched his hips, pushing his enormous cock through my flimsy silky barrier, stuffing me full, stealing my breath. Sharp pain ripped through me and I couldn't move.

Neither of us spoke for several long heartbeats, waiting for my shocked body to stretch and adjust to his size.

"Move with me, Salem," he whispered in my ear. He slid his cock slowly back and forth, stretching me wider and wider.

For several long breaths, I couldn't move, but then the friction of his flesh moving against mine sparked something inside me. I followed his rhythm, slow and steady, and the first unexpected, ungovernable pleasure rushed through my body, making me shiver.

And I found I wanted more. So much more.

Something took over me, a starving hunger.

Claim him. He's ours.

The voice whispered in my mind. At first, I didn't realize who it was but then my wolf flashed inside my head. It was her. She wanted him as much as I did.

Instinct took over. I locked my legs around him, drawing him to me, and increased the intensity of our rhythm, slamming my hips into his, taking him deeper and deeper inside me. Blood pounded between my temples and my legs in a crescendo. Pressure built up inside me until it exploded in an ecstasy of pleasure and I screamed, stars floating between my eyes. I scraped my fingers down the muscles rippling down his back, pulling him closer against me.

Mateo lifted his head and growled. "I claim you as mine forever."

In a loud voice, I called out, "And you're mine. I claim you as my mate." My commanding voice held power and I swear a pink aura glittered around us and then sank into us like a soft velvet blanket.

Mateo thrust one more time, emptying his hot seed inside me. Tingling sensations pushed through me culminating in a pool of unending pleasure. Waves of power glided through me, filling every core and every pore in a way that I couldn't even describe. I felt every shudder, every shift in our bodies until he collapsed on top of me, huffing and puffing as hard as I was, his hips still pumping.

I drew the words I wanted to say on his back, wishing I could speak them aloud. "What was that pink aura?" I panted. "Does that always happen in mating?"

"No, but there's something different about you, Salem—layers of secrets that I want to take a lifetime to uncover."

He nuzzled my neck. "I love you." His husky words were music to my ears and I sighed with contentment.

My heart quickened as I stroked his thick hair, feeling like the luckiest wolf in the world.

"Me, too." That was the closet I could get to saying those three little words.

He was mine and we were definitely mated. Someday I'd be able to say those words. My very last wall would come tumbling down and I would learn how to be that vulnerable.

But not today.

13

*M*ateo and I lay with our bodies entwined, still reeling from our mating. The sunlight heated our hot sleek bodies even more. I could happily have stayed like this all day but my tummy had other ideas. A loud, embarrassing growl rumbled through me.

He looked down at me with amusement. "Hungry, princess?"

My cheeks warmed. "I'm sorry."

"Don't be." He kissed my hot cheek. "Mating is hungry work." A wicked glint flashed in his eyes. "Or are you hungry for me?"

"I'm always hungry for you," I whispered. "But before we do another round of love making, I think I'd better get something to eat, or I won't survive."

"And I can't have that," he teased. He slowly pulled out of me and the stickiness of my blood mixed with his seed clung to my inner thighs.

"I need to shower first," I said as I rolled out of bed.

"Mind if I join you?" he asked.

I glanced cheekily over my shoulder. "I'd be disappointed if you didn't."

He clasped my hand and we walked into a luxurious marble

bathroom. He turned on the shower and kissed me all over, his hands moving along my quivering body, discovering every sensitive spot, turning me into a hot mess as steam filled the room.

I opened the frosted glass door and he followed me into the shower stall. Water splashed onto our heated bodies, creating even more steam. He crowded me against the marble wall, kissing me senseless. I slid my hand down his flat tummy, making him gasp.

I wrapped my fingers around his long shaft.

His eyes darkened. "Careful. You're walking into danger, princess." His voice was strained and I laughed, knowing I held him in my power.

"Promises, promises," I whispered. I slid my hand back and forth over his shaft as it pulsed in my palm.

He growled and grabbed my thighs, lifting me off the ground.

I gasped in surprise and immediately wrapped my arms around his neck to hold on tight. He arched his hips and drove his flesh deep into me again. It was easier this time. Wrapping my legs around him, I cried out with glee and kissed him, my tongue tangling with his. He thrust harder and harder and I matched his pounding rhythm until another wave of pleasure crashed over us.

I laid my head on his shoulder. Our heartbeats beat wildly and we stood there, him holding my trembling thighs and pressing my back against the wall until the water cooled.

Then my stomach let out another loud growl and the spell was broken.

He chuckled. "I guess I'd better get you something to eat."

I looked up at him and kissed him on the lips. "Blueberry pancakes?"

"Blueberry pancakes." He slowly lowered me to the ground. We rinsed off our bodies quickly as the water turned icy cold.

I was shivering as I grabbed us towels. We dried each other off and I delighted in memorizing his every contour, his every mole and freckle, his every scar. He was mine.

We came out of the shower, holding hands. He found a pair of sweats in a drawer and slowly put them on, hanging loosely on his hips. I threw on a pair of jeans and a sweater, but as I reached for the door to go down to breakfast, I stopped.

Shit, everyone would know what we had been doing.

He bumped into me. "Why did you stop? I thought you wanted blueberry pancakes."

I looked up at him. "But everyone will know what we were up to."

"Are you ashamed of what we just did?"

Beads of sweat broke out across my brow and I shifted from foot to foot. "No, it's just...I don't know..."

He lifted my chin and kissed my lips. "Supernaturals aren't like humans, Salem. We don't have the same archaic, prudish thoughts. Mating for us is life and power. It's what makes us stronger." His voice calmed my nerves and I exhaled slowly.

He opened the door and stretched out his hand. "Come with me."

Shaking, I clasped his hand and he led me out of the bedroom. With each step we took, blood pumped to my face making it hotter and hotter. I'm sure my face was turning redder than my hair.

Dread filled me, nearly choking my throat. I even pulled back a little, but Mateo would have none of it and gently tugged me down the stairs.

Everyone was sitting around the living room talking until they saw us. Then they fell silent.

Queen Gwendoline broke into a big smile. "Ah, I see our new queen has chosen her king."

This time, it was Mateo's turn to stop and I bumped into him.

"What?" Shock gripped his voice.

I stared at his stiff back, wondering if he regretted mating with me. I remembered he had talked about rejected mates. All of my memories of foster care came crashing back, nearly knocking me on my ass. God, why had I listened to my wolf? I should have remained alone like always.

I wiggled my hand, trying to get free, but he only squeezed tighter.

The queen looked at him, confused. "You've mated, have you not?"

"Yes." Mateo pulled me forward and wrapped his arm securely around my waist as if to announce what we had done.

A red balloon of shame burst on my cheeks and I almost buried my face in his naked chest.

Ashton looked at me and gave me a smile. "You have nothing to be ashamed of, Salem. This is our way. Indeed, you are to be congratulated for finding your mate."

I thought I detected a note of regret in his voice. Mateo must have heard it too because his arm tightened around me.

"She wants blueberry pancakes," Mateo said gruffly.

"I'll make some." Quint started to get out of the recliner but Mateo stopped him.

"No, I want to make them for her. Do you have blueberries?"

Quint sat back down. "Of course, in the refrigerator."

Mateo led me down the stairs but the queen blocked our way. She was almost a foot shorter than Mateo but she was a force to be reckoned with. She put her hand on his broad chest. "You do not want to be her king?"

He blurted, "I didn't say that. But I'm not royalty. How can I be king?"

She dropped her hand. "Times are changing, Mateo. Royalty can take whoever they like as their mate. King Gunnar set a precedent when he chose Ebony as his queen. She was not born royal."

Mateo laughed. "I think people would challenge you on that. She's the daughter of the Golden Phoenix and some consider him royalty."

"But he's not," the queen corrected gently. "He's a well-respected, brave warrior as are his daughters and his mate, but like you, they were not born royal. Nevertheless, Ebony is the current queen of the Dark Demons."

"Still—"

"You're a great warrior yourself," Ashton piped up. "You put your life at risk to restore the missing princess to her rightful throne."

I slipped around him and looked up at him. "And you still are. You're still being hunted, like me. You've saved my life more than once. What more could a queen ask for?"

"But the old guard…" his voice trailed off.

"Will have a difficult time accepting this, yes," the queen finished for him. "There will those who will oppose it—"

"Like my father," Ashton grumbled.

Queen Gwendoline gave him a thoughtful look. "Your father might surprise you, Ashton. King Christopher is steeped in the old ways, but he's also a man of honor. He believes that good is stronger than evil. And if I'm not mistaken, he's one of the few kings that has so far acknowledged Queen Ebony. That says a lot about his character and his ability to change."

Ashton pulled his eyebrows tight together as if to argue, but then his face relaxed. "I guess you're right. I never thought about it that way."

"You've painted a rather black picture of your father in your mind, Ashton. Give him half a chance and I think you'll find he'll become one of your biggest allies."

Mateo gave the queen an incredulous look. "You actually think a king will accept a mere guard as an equal?"

She clasped his arm. "Yes, I do. Mind you, not all will. Even among royalty there are those that think they are above everyone else."

"You mean like my uncle?" I blurted out.

"He's one of them," she said grimly. "Ryker was like that too, and had allies who thought as he did. He felt so strongly about it, he went to war."

A shudder of fear went down my back. What if our mating was going to open up another can of worms? I didn't want to be responsible for bringing on another supernatural war, but I wasn't going to give up Mateo, either.

"That's not exactly comforting," Mateo mumbled.

"I refuse to lose you." I needed to distract him. "But right now, I want blueberry pancakes."

His frown melted away and he tapped a single finger on my nose. "You have a one-track mind."

I rubbed my grumbling belly. "When I'm hungry, I do."

"Come on, then." He tilted his head. "Let's feed you."

We went into the kitchen and he pointed to a bar stool. "Sit."

"I can help."

"No helping. I want to make you pancakes."

I rolled my eyes but was secretly touched that he wanted to do this for me. This would be the second time he'd cooked me breakfast.

He opened the refrigerator and pulled out blueberries, eggs, milk, butter, and sour cream. Next, he found a mixing bowl.

"Do you actually know how to make blueberry pancakes without a recipe?"

"You're not going to believe this, but my team liked me to cook breakfast, and they really liked pancakes."

I cocked my eyebrow. "Really? I would have thought they would prefer meat."

"In wolf form, we only eat meat..." He winked and gave me a big ol' grin. "But we're not always wolves."

There were canisters on the marble counter and he checked them. "Ah good, flour and sugar." He opened the pantry and pulled out a can of baking powder. He mixed all the ingredients in the bowl.

I inhaled the smell of freshly-brewed coffee and my mouth began to water.

Mateo followed my gaze. "Would you like a cup of coffee, beautiful?"

"Mm, yes." I started to get off my stool, but he gently pushed me back down.

I frowned. "What are you doing?"

"Taking care of you."

I lifted my chin. "I can take care of myself."

"I know." He gently pushed me down on the chair. "But maybe this time, just let me take care of you."

I sighed heavily. "Because I'm the missing wolf princess?"

"No, my stubborn one." He clasped my chin and brushed his lips over mine. "Because I love you and you're my mate. Is that so bad?"

My mouth ran dry. He was slowly chipping away at my carefully-built wall. I wanted to utter those three words so badly. They were right on the tip of my tongue. But fear froze them there.

All I could do was brush my lips over his and wrap my arms around his neck, pressing my chest against his, hoping he could feel the love swelling in my heart.

14

*M*ateo fixed the best blueberry pancakes I had ever had. Or maybe it was because he made them specially for me. No guy had ever done that before.

"Those were so good, huh Hades?" I finished my last bite, the blueberries bursting in my mouth.

The little Catalan dragon ignored me. He was far too busy greedily lapping up the last of his plate of syrup and blueberry pancakes.

Mateo grinned. "Glad you both liked them."

Queen Gwendoline came into the kitchen. "So, Salem, are you ready to study the Book of Goody?"

My gut tumbled and the pancakes turned to stone in my belly.

Mateo squeezed my hand. "You can do this, Salem." His reassurance didn't calm my nerves. They were wound up tighter than a guitar string.

I nodded, unsure. The last time I cast a spell from that book I'd ended up in a coma.

But I wasn't going to give up, either. I pushed my chair away from the table. "Okay, let's do this. But first I'll help Mateo with the dishes."

Quint walked past the queen. "No, that's my job." He tilted his head. "Go with the queen."

I almost wanted to argue, not because I especially wanted to do the dishes, but because I wanted to postpone studying the Book of Goody.

Then again, if I wanted to defeat Calvin, I had to master it.

I took a deep breath and pushed my chair away from the table. "Fine. Lead on."

Mateo clasped my hand. Hades licked his lips, shook out his mane, and followed right on my heels as always. The three of us followed Queen Gwendoline into the living room where Remi was reading a book and Ashton was dozing in the recliner.

Hades snarled.

Ashton woke with a start and looked around wildly. "What? What's wrong?" Sleep was still in the corner of his eyes.

"Hades," I chided. "You didn't have to wake him like that."

Hades sat down on his haunches and gave me an apologetic look. I couldn't help but laugh and rubbed his cheeks with my palms. "It's okay, buddy. You're forgiven."

Ashton glared but didn't counter me.

Queen Gwendoline spread out her arms. "Except for Salem and me, everyone else take a seat. Salem, come and stand here."

I stared at the Book of Goody. My insides turned uneasily and I wished I hadn't eaten so much.

"You'll be fine." Mateo rubbed my back, his touch easing some of my fear. But I couldn't shake the feeling he might be wrong. And what then?

"Now." Queen Gwendoline put her hand on my shoulder. "I think you will find you're stronger, Salem, when you use the spell book this time. Mating always makes us stronger."

I nodded, not quite believing what she had just said, but what the hell.

Queen Gwendoline whispered in my ear, "You can do this,

Salem. Don't be afraid. Your pack is here, and they will give you power. So will your mate."

I looked over my shoulder at her serene face. "What spell am I supposed to learn?"

"Look inside you and think of the spell you'll need when you and your team free Gloria."

"Don't you mean try to free Gloria?" Mateo's voice was filled with dread and despair.

"No, I don't. I have complete faith in all of you." Queen Gwendoline met his uneasy gaze levelly. The confidence in her voice gave me the courage to take a step toward the Book of Goody.

My legs trembled but that didn't stop me. I picked up the book.

Trust me

That same voice whispered through my mind like a soft breeze and I silently whispered back.

We need to help Gloria

I put my palm on top of the book. My heart thundered, sending power through me. The same familiar tingling sensations rushed through me, ten times stronger than the last time. Wind blew my hair around me faster and faster. This time I was definitely stronger, I could feel it. Pink sparkles flittered around my fingers and seeped into the cover.

A tingling force moved through me as my fingers riffled through the pages and then stopped. I looked at the page they had landed on—Moresco Horrendegris.

The voice whispered in my mind again, not quite so softly this time. Hurry. Time is running out.

Mateo sat on the edge of his chair. "What does it say?"

I skimmed the page. "It looks like a location spell."

The queen looked down and read over my shoulder. "You're right. It is."

Ashton frowned. "Why would the book show you that?

Wouldn't Calvin keep Gloria in his secret room, same as Mateo and me?"

"If you recall," the queen said, "both of you escaped. Calvin is very shrewd. If his secret room has been discovered, he would move his prisoners."

I rubbed my sweaty forehead. "So, that means Hayley too?"

"I'm afraid so," the queen said. "We have to hope that she and Gloria are together."

"That's not likely," Mateo interjected. "Besides, Calvin's upping his game and getting even more dangerous. We need to proceed with great caution."

"I agree," Remi said. "He's a bastard, and a crafty one. Knowing him, he'll come up with some evil plan to lead us straight to him."

I looked at the queen. "Do you think I should try a different spell?"

"Well, what does your gut tell you?"

I closed my eyes. My wolf pushed through and the look in her green eyes was unmistakable. I opened my eyes again and took deep breath. "No."

"Then stop for now. When you need a spell, the book will have one, but like Anton warned you, you must not do too many because it will take a toll on you." She smiled. "Even if you are now mated. Magic is very powerful and you must build up a tolerance to using it. Even the most powerful witch starts out small."

"There was something else I felt..." I hesitated, not sure if I should tell Ashton.

"What?" He stood, his eyes filling with anxiety. "It's about Gloria, isn't it?" Dread shook his voice.

I swallowed back my hesitation and met his despairing look. His shoulders drooped and his face had paled.

"Tell me," he urged.

I couldn't lie. "There's a voice I always hear when I use the Book of Goody. It's the magic, I think..."

He took a step toward me. "And?"

I bit my lip. "It said time was running out."

"Then we have to go now."

We all looked at each other uncertainly.

Ashton gritted his teeth. "Look, if you're all going to stand around here with your thumbs up your asses, fine. But not me. I'm not going to let her die."

Mateo stepped in front of him. "And how are you going to find her?"

Ashton shoved him. "I don't know, but I will."

"Ashton," I said softly. "We'll all go, but we can't just storm out of here. That's what Calvin wants. We have to have a plan. I haven't even used the location spell yet."

He ran his hands through his hair. "Then use it, Salem. Gloria's life depends on it." His angry voice said he was about to shift and lose control.

I held up both my palms. "I will, I promise, but please, you need to calm down."

Hades stepped in front of me, snarling.

Ashton looked between him, me, and Mateo. Quint had stepped back into the living room. His dark just-try-and-get-past-me-dude scowl said he was one step away from vamping out.

Muttering under his breath, Ashton reluctantly sat down again.

Mateo gestured toward me with his hand. "Continue."

I nodded and inhaled and exhaled deeply several times until the tension in my muscles lessened.

In a soft voice, I said, "Moresco Horrendegris."

Pink smoke snaked out of the book and then swept up my nose. My back arched and my arms flew wide. My body shook uncontrollably.

"Salem—" Mateo cried.

"No. Stay back," the queen said, stopping him. "Watch. Learn."

Their voices sounded like they were somewhere far away. Or maybe it was me…

Brown, red, white, and purple colors spun around in my vision. Suddenly, they stopped. I was outside a dilapidated single story stone cabin next to a lake with a wraparound deck. The door hung ajar and I slipped inside as if I were a ghost. The place was a shambles and books, candles, and broken pieces of ceramic littered the hardwood floor. The red leather sofa and matching love seat had deep claw marks in the upholstery, exposing moldy stuffing and rusty springs.

Crap, I knew where I was. This was the witch Hayley's cabin.

I noticed a bookcase that had been shoved aside, revealing a stairwell that went downstairs. I never noticed that the last time I was in here. God, that seemed so long ago.

Every instinct told me they were down there. I inhaled, nearly choking on a foul stench of death. Somehow, I forced myself to descend the stairs step by cautious step.

Clop Clop Clop Clop

I got a whiff of another scent—wolf.

At the bottom of the stairs, I gasped. Gloria and Hayley were strung up like a couple of Thanksgiving turkeys. Their arms were stretched over their heads and their blond hair was tangled. Dirt stained their faces. There were holes in Gloria's blue gown, and huge rips in Hayley's T-shirt and jeans. I couldn't imagine what they had gone through.

"Salem, at last. We've been waiting for you."

Velkan and the demon wolves stepped out of the shadows. "I have what you're looking for." He held the Rose Box, supposedly containing all the evidence that proved my uncle killed my parents.

I caught a glimpse of something moving in the shadows behind him.

Something that didn't want to be seen.

Something evil.

D ark and light colors spun around me again, and I stumbled backward, screaming.

Strong arms caught me. "Salem, Salem. Answer me."

My eyes fluttered open. Mateo carried me to a couch and lay me down, stroking my hair and holding me close, but I couldn't stop trembling. I inhaled his scent that eased the horrible stench somewhat. His steady heartbeat calmed my frantic one.

I looked up into Mateo's dark eyes, grounding myself in his presence. I took another deep breath. "Mateo, I know...." I balled my fists into his shirt. "...I know where they are."

"Where?" Ashton demanded.

I turned away from Mateo's gaze and met Ashton's intense stare.

"Tell me." Ashton knelt in front of me. "She's my mate." He lowered his head. "I should have claimed her. She'd have been safe at Highburn Fortress."

I cleared the dust bunnies from my throat. "She's at the witch's cabin by the lake."

Remi's eyes widened and she put her hand on her chest. "You don't mean the witch's cabin by my home?"

Ashton's drew his brows together and his eyes shone with disbelief. "You mean Hayley's home? Are you sure?"

"Absolutely," I said. "But that's not all."

They're being guarded?"

"That goes without saying," Mateo said.

"You don't understand—by Velkan and the demon wolves."

Mateo gritted his teeth. "Shit."

"Even that's not the worst of it," I continued. "They know we're coming."

"How do you know?" Ashton asked.

I cleared my throat, trying to sound like I was more in control than I felt. "Because somehow Velkan was able to see me. He has the Rose Box. It's almost like he was taunting me with it."

Ashton stared at me with huge, worried eyes. "Was Gloria okay?"

I looked down at my feet. The image of her and Hayley strung up still made my heart race. How could I tell them what I had seen?

Ashton clasped my arms. "Salem, answer me."

I lifted my head and sighed heavily. "I—I don't know. She and Hayley were both unconscious and chained to a wall."

"Had she been tortured?" His pained voice made me want to fudge the truth.

Then I blinked and thought about it for a couple of deep breaths. No, I couldn't lie to him. "I...don't know. She and Hayley were both filthy but I didn't see any bruises or blood."

"He could have used dark magic on them. He might have forced Hayley to use whatever magic is in the Rose Box on them," Queen Gwendoline said sadly.

"Damn it." Ashton sat on the floor in defeat. "How the hell are we going to get into that place? Only Salem and Hades were ever able to."

I blurted, "That's not all."

Ashton looked up. "What?"

"There was something behind them, a dark presence I couldn't quite see. I got the feeling it was hiding from me."

Remi's face paled. "Calvin?"

I shrugged miserably. "I don't know."

Mateo shook his head. "I knew this was going to happen. Calvin has a set a damn trap. There's no fucking way we can come out of this alive."

I caught Queen Gwendoline's knowing gaze. We had just talked about why I shouldn't cast any more spells but my options were nil. I so didn't want to do this, but I stared at the Book of

Goody. "A spell. I could look for one that would allow other super-naturals to enter, not just me and Hades."

Mateo tightened his arms around me. "No. You know what happened last time."

I looked up at him. "Would you rather Hades and I fight Velkan and the demon wolves on our own?"

His eyes darkened and his body tensed. "Of course not, but another spell? Are you sure?"

I cupped his rugged face. "Do you have any other suggestions?"

He didn't answer me. There was no other way and he knew it.

Unless I wanted to take on a demon and the demon wolves by myself.

But even that wasn't the only problem. There was that dark presence waiting for me that could even be worse.

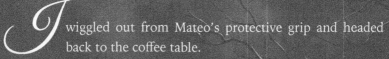

wiggled out from Mateo's protective grip and headed back to the coffee table.

"Salem, wait." Mateo reached for me but I evaded him.

Remi stepped in front of the coffee table and put her hands on my shoulders. "Are you sure about this, honey? Remember what happened last time."

I wasn't sure about it at all, but the alternative was that only Hades and I went into that cabin, and everything told me that would definitely be a mistake.

Squaring my shoulders, I looked into her fear-stricken face. "I can do this, Remi."

"Be careful." She dropped her arms and stepped aside.

I brushed past her and picked up the Book of Goody. It trembled in my hands.

Ask me, the voice whispered in my mind.

Please help us to break the spell guarding the cabin and to retrieve the Rose Box.

Nothing happened.

Did you hear me?

The clock chimed several times on the grandfather clock in the living room. I wasn't sure if the voice would answer. Finally it did.

It could be dangerous. Then every supernatural can enter the house. Is that really what you want? Rather than confident, the voice sounded frail and fearful.

Oh, God. This was definitely not good.

I can't do this alone. I need my pack.

Very well, the voice answered.

Once again, I spread my fingers over the leather. When the sensations rushed through me the wind was icy this time, making me shiver. Pink sparkles swirled around my palm and that same tugging sensation led me to turn the pages, flicking through the book and stopping quite far through it.

Shit, this meant the spell was even more powerful. Could I even handle it?

The voice didn't answer me, which was another bad sign.

In bold letters at the top of the page was the word Isois. Below was a short paragraph that said it could counter a witch's protection spell, but there was also a warning that this was a high-level skill, and it could easily go awry.

"Did you find a spell?" Mateo asked.

I wouldn't lie to my mate, even though I know it was going to lead to a battle. "I did, but it's a really advanced one and I'm not sure I'm strong enough yet to use it."

"Then don't," he said simply.

I put the book back on the coffee table. "So, you want me to fight—"

"No," he said, a little too loudly for my taste.

I narrowed my eyes. "Then what?" I asked quietly.

Mateo looked at each of us. "We come up with a different plan. Maybe we can draw Velkan and the demon wolves out of the cabin and give you and Hades a chance to go in and rescue Gloria and Hayley—"

"What about the presence lurking in the darkness?" I broke in.

He lowered his head. "I don't know," he said miserably.

"May I make a suggestion?" The queen stepped in front of us as if she were anxious to avert World War Three.

"What?" Mateo and I both answered at once.

"I wouldn't rush headlong into the cabin."

Ashton paced the room. "But what about Gloria and Hayley? They could die in there."

"Maybe," she said. "Tell me, Mateo, what would you do in a situation like this? If you were planning to rescue a captured comrade?"

He rubbed his chin. "We would send out a reconnaissance team to gather more information," he admitted.

Her eyes sparkled. "Exactly."

"I could do it." Quint's low voice made me jump.

I hadn't even heard him come into the living room.

He looked at each of us. "They don't know me. I could get there faster than any of you. How far is this place from here?"

Remi thought about it for a minute. "About a hundred miles to the south. It's near my home. But surely Calvin's having my place watched."

Quint frowned. "You keep mentioning this Rose Box. What is it?"

"It's a wooden box with hand-carved roses on it, about the size of a shoe box," I said. "According to the witch Hayley, there is proof inside that my uncle killed my parents and forced the witch to do his dirty work, information that tells where the last archives are hidden, and instructions how to break the Unseelie spell controlling the demon wolves."

Quint lifted his eyebrow. "Archives?"

"Supposedly, hidden in the archives is the source of the first king's power. Calvin is desperate to find it."

"Wouldn't Calvin have opened the box by now?" he asked.

I shook my head. "He can't. It's enchanted."

Mateo shrugged. "I guess Quint could scope the place out first. It will take us at least a couple of days to get there by wolf."

"If only Raven was here," I muttered.

"She and Lucien are busy helping the new king and queen of the Dark Demons. This is your fight," the queen said. "I also must return to my kingdom soon. My son Rhys is anxious to find his beloved and I must ensure he is not doing anything rash."

Mateo scanned the living room. "Do you have a Colorado map? I can show you where the cabin is located. It's just north of the town of Frisco, between there and Leadville."

"I know where that is. I can get there in less than three hours. One second."

Quint returned shortly with a map and Mateo pointed to a spot. "This is where Remi's cabin is. The witch's cabin is cloaked but there's a little lake west of her place with a large boulder next to it. The lake and her cabin are right adjacent to it."

"I'll find it." He looked at each of us. "I'll also pack a bag of clothes for each of you for when you shift back into your human forms, unless you want to run around in your birthday suits."

"Not especially," I chuckled. Fighting naked wasn't at the top of my list.

"What happens when we get there and we can't get into the cabin?" Ashton asked. "Should Salem use her spell?"

The queen held our gaze. "Breaking another witch's spell is very costly physically for the one who breaks it. If she performs this spell, her magic will be depleted temporarily."

"Damn it," Mateo grumbled. "This just fucking gets better and better."

"I don't think she should use it unless it's absolutely necessary," Remi said. "If she gets into a weakened state, they could capture her. I will not lose Salem to Calvin like I did her mother and father."

Mateo puffed out his chest. "I won't let that happen."

"I don't think we can make any decisions until we see what's really going on," I said. "We all need to remain calm." I looked down at the Book of Goody and an unsettling feeling made my skin prickle. "Should we leave the book here unguarded?"

The queen got a pensive look. "I don't know. Why don't you ask it?"

My eyes widened. I put my hand on the cover again and a tremor went up my arm.

No, take me with you. You need me. I can help you get the Rose Box.

The voice sounded desperate and frightened, as if it didn't want to be alone.

"Well?" Mateo asked.

I removed my hand from the quivering book. "It definitely comes with us. I think the book can help us retrieve the Rose Box, but I can't carry it as a wolf."

"Don't worry," Quint said. "I can. I'll guard it to the bitter end." His ominous tone sent a shiver through me. I just hoped it didn't get that far.

"So we have a plan," Mateo said. "I suggest we get ready and leave today."

"I'm with you on that," Ashton chimed in.

For the next hour, we collected the clothes, coats, and shoes that we wanted Quint to bring and we hurried up to the guard tower. The Book of Goody was safely tucked away in the bundle of clothes and I hoped it would be safe. By the time we were done, the bag was bulging at the seams.

I looked at the bag and then at Quint. "Are you sure you can carry that?"

He gave me a wily smile. "You've seen my bat, haven't you?"

I nodded.

He gripped my shoulder. "So don't fret, princess. I can carry twice that load."

From the guard tower, I scanned the breathtaking view of the

Rocky Mountains and valleys. It was beautiful and I could see why Anton loved it here. Hades nudged closer to me.

A cool breeze brushed over me, sending my hair flying. "What about this place? Will anyone be able to break in?"

He dropped his hand and shook his head. "It's well warded. Anton didn't spare any expense in protecting his hideaway."

I put a hand on his broad chest. "Be careful, Quint."

He winked. "I will. Stand back."

We did as he asked, giving him plenty of space. He shifted into his huge bat, twice as big as a bald eagle. He swooped down and easily grabbed the bag in his talons. He soared into the deep blue sky, carrying our things as if they weighed nothing.

"Be safe, friend," I whispered.

Hades growled and snarled, as if echoing my sympathies.

Mateo put an arm around my shoulders. "He will be fine. Quint's one tough bastard. Velkan and the demon wolves will think twice before attacking him."

"I hope so." I leaned my head on his shoulder, watching Quint slowly disappear into the sky.

"We should get going." Ashton couldn't hide the impatience in his voice.

For once, I was going to indulge him. I eased away from Mateo. "Are we all ready?"

Everyone nodded, including Hades, determination in their eyes. My wolf pushed against me, wanting to be released.

I led them out of the tower. "Then let's do this."

We headed down the stairwell and made for the front door that led out to the snow-covered courtyard. The sun cast shadows on the ground and a chill was in the air. The drawbridge, the only way into the fortress, was at the end of the courtyard.

"I'll lower the drawbridge while you all shift," Mateo said.

"Hades, please stay and help Mateo get over the bridge."

"I can do it myself."

I shook my head. "So stubborn."

We all stripped out of our clothes. My wolf trembled with excitement. She was ready for battle, even if I wasn't. My bones and muscles changed and contorted until I was my beautiful white wolf, taller and broader than Ashton's gray wolf and Remi's red one.

Mateo lowered the drawbridge. My wolf panted with excitement.

AAAaaaaaaooo

Ashton and Remi answered my call.

She was ready to run free and her excitement fueled mine.

Once the drawbridge was lowered and the gate opened, I burst through the wooden door like a soaring cannon.

Creak Creak Clank Clank

The drawbridge slowly rose up again. Hades flew up in the air. Mateo's black wolf clawed its way up, but just as Hades was going to grab him, Mateo jumped. He missed his landing and rolled in the snow.

Dammit!

I hurried over to him, sniffing and nosing around him to ensure he was okay. He immediately got up and gave me a I'm-fine irritated shake of his head. I nuzzled his neck, telling him I loved him, but then I nipped out his ear to remind him who was boss. He whimpered into submission.

Hades landed next to him and snapped his jaw.

Mateo growled, but didn't attack, which was smart. Hades might be small but the little guy could pack a wallop harder than one from the Incredible Hulk.

I stepped back and howled.

Aaaaaoooo

My pack joined me in the we're-coming song. Hades joined too, letting out a mighty roar. Our voices were mournful and sad, as if we knew some of us might not be coming back. But we weren't backing down.

I looked at each of them in turn and bolted into the woods,

heading back to the witch's cabin. I raced around trees, flew over branches and rocks. Birds tweeted and chirped overhead as if to send a message to everyone that we were on the move.

Deer scattered when they saw us, terrified that we were out for a meal, but we weren't interested in them. Not today anyway.

The snow was deep and sometimes I sank into it up to my chest, but I plowed through the white stuff, refusing to give up.

My team fanned out behind me, keeping up the frantic pace, while Hades flew overhead as our lookout, swooping over and under tree limbs. The journey ahead would be long, but adrenaline pumped through me. This was going to be a showdown between good and evil and this time, I wouldn't be hiding in the shadows.

Velkan said they were waiting for me.

The question was—were they ready for the Vindicators?

16

We didn't stop to rest until the sun slid behind the mountains. The temperature had dropped and snow was falling around us, blinding my vision. I was glad for my warm fur, but I needed to get my pack out of the snow. Our bellies were empty and we needed meat.

I sniffed the air and caught the scent of deer. I turned to look at my pack and they knew instantly what I wanted. We divided up as we approached our prey that was hiding between the trees. It was a lone doe and I could sense her fear. I felt momentarily sorry for her, but we were hungry predators, and she shouldn't have left her herd.

I'd never killed anything before and would have hesitated, but my wolf didn't have a problem with it. Mateo and Ashton attacked from the rear. The doe bolted, but she slid into my path. I lunged, my teeth sinking into her throat. Blood burst into my mouth and slid down my throat. With one strike, I had killed her.

The human inside me recoiled but my wolf was starving. We all were. The whole pack, including Hades, feasted on the poor doe, tearing into the meat. Once our bellies were full, we curled up in a grove of pine trees and rested. Mateo curled up around me and Hades laid in front of me. I was glad for my two protectors, but I kept scanning the frozen tundra, worried that our enemies would hunt us down.

The wind rustled over us, stirring our fur. Snow swirled around us like we were inside a snow globe. I kept lifting my head and sniffing, but Mateo's steady heartbeat reminded me of the soothing song from the *Phantom of the Opera* "Music of the Night", and it lulled me to sleep.

"...Let the dream begin, let your darker side give in
To the power of the music that I write
The power of the music of the night..."

The song played over and over in my mind. I went to see a matinee performance of *Phantom of the Opera* with one of my group homes once, and I fell in love with it. "Music of the Night" had been my favorite song from it, and my heartbeat fell into sync with Mateo's. My eyelids fluttered heavily until I couldn't keep them open any longer and I feel asleep, huddling next to Mateo and Hades and dreaming of dancing with the Phantom who looked exactly like Mateo.

Something furry nuzzled my neck. I opened my eyes to stare into Mateo's dark ones. The darkness had faded and the sky was slowly turning pink and orange. Ashton, Remi, and Hades were all waiting for me. I got up immediately, not believing they let me sleep so long. I stretched out, arching my back and wagging my tail.

Ashton paced back and forth as if he was anxious to leave. I couldn't make him wait any longer.

I sniffed the air and scented deer hiding deep in the forest, but I didn't detect any other predators nearby, especially demon ones.

What I did feel was that something was pulling me toward it, calling through the dense woods. I couldn't tell if the something was good or evil. All I knew was that I had to go to it.

Once again, I led my team, my paws pounding over the snow. We moved faster and faster, barely touching the ground, until gradually I began to recognize the terrain. By the time I slowed our pace, the sun was starting to set again. High up on a cliff, we looked down onto the busy buzzing cars on I-70 full of skiers eager to hit the slopes. Off of I-70 was the town of Frisco, right next to Lake Dillon that supplied Denver's drinking water.

Remi's home was just to the north. It was off a beaten path, far away from the nearby mountain towns of Dillon and Silverton that only had a couple of houses apiece. Excitement flushed through me at the thought of seeing it again. I loved that little A-frame cabin. It was the first time any place felt like home. I got a pang when I considered that Calvin might not have even allowed it to remain standing.

I led my pack away from the busy roads and highways, preferring to stay close to the trees, aspens, and bushes, trying not to be seen by human or, worse, supernatural eyes. Finally, we reached the dirt road Mateo had taken me down on his motorcycle when he'd come to my unit at Sunshine Trailers and saved me from the assassins Calvin had sent to kill me. That seemed a whole other lifetime ago.

We still had another couple of miles to go if we wanted to get to safety without being seen. Suddenly we stopped to smell and I cringed. A jolt of dread shot through me, knotting my shoulders, and making my hackles stand straight up. I pulled back my upper lip and growled softly. Wolves and vampires were here. Wolves and vampires that were definitely in league with Calvin.

And there was something else, something I had never detected before, but whatever it was it had an evil taint to it. I wanted to ask what it was, but being in wolf form, I couldn't speak.

Mateo nudged me and by the look in his eyes, he wanted me

and the others to follow him. Rather than going down the little gravel road, he led us into the woods, taking a trail that ran parallel to it. Excitement and dread pumped through me with each step we took.

Please let the house be standing

Then my blood ran cold.

Thump Thump Thump

Heavy footsteps crunched on the snow as they approached. My ears flattened back and my hackles stood up. I pulled my upper lip back into the meanest snarl I could muster. Hades and Mateo came up alongside me, snarling and growling. Ashton and Remi were protecting the rear.

A large man was heading toward us, carrying what looked like an oversized suitcase. Hades lunged, forward his tail wagging. He circled the man happily like a dog would his owner.

I inhaled and stopped growling. I recognized the scent.

Quint.

His heavy boots crunched the snow with every step. The sunlight highlighted his wavy brown hair and he had on leather pants that clung to his muscular legs and a buttoned-up duster. Dark sunglasses hid his eyes. He looked something out of *The Matrix*.

Scowling, he tossed the bag in front of us. "It's about time you all got here." But then his frown melted away into a big ol' grin. "I was getting lonely."

I shifted first, needing to know the *Book of Goody* was safe inside. "What's been going on?" I could barely get the words out, my teeth were chattering so much.

My nipples budded from the freezing cold and goosebumps broke out all over me. I grabbed my undergarments and whipped them on, followed by my thick blue sweater and a pair of jeans. I grinned when I saw the *Book of Goody* safe and sound. I pulled on my socks and boots and then slid into my coat.

"Lots. First, Remi's house was burned to the ground. There's not much left of it, except for the training room. That's intact."

My heart sank. Tears slid down my cheeks and I bit back a sob. I don't know why this upset me so much but I suppose it was because once again, I had lost something that was precious to me. Damn Calvin.

"I'm sorry," Quint said.

Mateo knelt next me, still naked, and pulled me into his arms. His spicy masculine scent eased some of the pain. I should have let him get dressed but I clung to him, needing to feel his warmth and strength. Calvin had taken so much from me and I knew he wasn't done—not by a long shot.

He cradled me close. "We'll rebuild, don't worry. Right now, we have to save Gloria and Hayley."

I pulled away and wiped my tears. "Sorry. He's just...just..."

He cocked his eyebrow and grinned. "A bastard?"

"And then some."

Remi stood away from us. She had already dressed and stood with her arms folded and head lowered. Her shoulders were shaking.

I slowly approached her. "Remi?"

She turned around. Tears had frozen to her cheeks but it was the loss and despair in her eyes that really broke my heart. I ran to her and we hugged each other tightly, both at a complete loss for words. My heart thundered, sending blood pumping between my ears. Hers was beating just as hard as mine, threatening to explode with fury and pain.

"I'm sorry," I whispered in her ears. "I'm so sorry."

Hades plopped down beside us and sighed heavily.

She untangled herself from me and wiped her cheeks. "It's just I always felt safe there. Everything I owned was in that place. All the pictures of your parents...all the mementos..." She snapped her fingers. "And just like that Calvin took it all away from me. Again."

"I know. It was the first place that felt like home to me." My voice choked and I thought I'd burst into tears again.

Calvin didn't just hurt people. He destroyed their lives. He took everything away. He'd done it to Remi, and Hayley, and now, Gloria. His own daughter.

God, was I powerful enough to defeat such a man? Was he even a man?

Mateo came up behind me and wrapped his arms around me, not saying anything. His presence gave me strength to regain control, to be the leader I was born to be.

I took a sobering breath and leaned into him, feeling his heartbeat against my back. I put my hands on his arm. "I'm okay."

He kissed the back of my neck. "Good. You'll beat him, Salem. I know you will. I have faith in you."

Mateo quickly got dressed, putting on a pair of black jeans, a black sweater, a leather jacket and a pair of boots. He looked like he did the first day I met him when he saved me from the assassins. He had struck me as an ultimate bad boy then—and now he was all mine.

Quint looked at each one of us. "Now, that you're all decent... I'll tell you what I've learned, but not here. I think we should retreat to Remi's bunker. Calvin's goons have assumed that with the home literally burned to the ground nobody will take shelter there." He tilted his head. "Follow me."

Remi and I locked hands as we followed Quint through the forest. She was still trembling. He took us to what had once been Remi's beautiful A-frame home. Nothing was left except the scorched foundation.

Remi released a tortured sob and I hugged her again. She buried her face against my shoulder, crying silently. I stroked her hair and rubbed her back, trying to stop my own tears, but they wouldn't be denied.

Hades wrapped his body around us as if trying to comfort us.

"We must get below quickly," Quint said. "Patrols might come by here any minute. Lucky for us the snow will soon cover your footprints."

"Yes, come on," Mateo urged. "We need to go."

I allowed him to lead me. We followed Quint down the stairs below the burnt foundation that still smelled of ash and smoke. Quint opened the door and took us downstairs. It was strangely intact. None of the mirrors had been broken and the mats had been rolled out, perhaps used for bedding.

Remi hurried over to a wall and pressed on a wolf etched into it. A secret panel opened to a room containing not only swords, bows and arrows and crossbows, but also a generator.

"At least they didn't find this," she murmured. She pulled on the cord several times and the generator rumbled to life. Lights flickered on in the bunker.

Ashton frowned. "How come they didn't get in here?"

She entered the room. "Because only my palm print will open the door." She stepped inside and pressed a small medallion on the panel. Another wall slid open.

My eyes widened, taking in the secret room.

Remi scanned the room. "Good. Everything's here and working perfectly. This is my safe house. I have food, a small stove, and a microwave in here. In case Calvin found me, I wanted to be ready for a siege."

I looked through the doorway. "I never knew this was even here." There was a freezer softly humming, a refrigerator, cabinets, a small sink, even a modest shower in the corner. It was amazing.

Mateo came up behind me. "Smart. Very smart, Remi. I've got a feeling we may very well be holed up down here if Calvin finds out where we are."

17

Quint scanned the contents in the store room. "You could have told me this place was here. I've been living on animals." Anger simmered beneath his tone.

Remi looked at him. "Why? There's no blood bags. And you wouldn't have been able to get in here, anyway."

An amused smile flashed across his lips. "I may have one or two abilities you don't know about."

That intrigued me. "Like what?"

"I'm one of the few vampires that can shift into smoke."

"What else can you tell us? What's been going on?" Ashton asked.

"From what I can tell, besides Velkan and his demon wolves, there are dark demon and Unseelies renegades here."

I remembered the sinister presence in my vision. "Anything else?"

"I haven't seen anything come out of the witch's cabin, but there's definitely something inside. Something evil, though I don't know what it is."

Quint confirmed my worst fears. I stroked Hades' mane. "So,

Hades and I will be walking into an unknown danger, perhaps a deadly one."

Mateo growled. "No. I'm not letting you go in there alone."

Hades growled.

"I won't be alone. This little guy will be with me."

"That's not enough," Mateo said. "We need to draw out whatever is in the witch's cabin."

I frowned. "How?"

He held my gaze. "Live bait."

"You're thinking of yourself, aren't you?"

"Who better to draw them out than a traitorous guard? Calvin would consider it a coup if he could recapture me."

I put my hands on his broad chest, feeling his thumping heart. "Don't you think I'm the better prize?"

He gently clasped my wrists. "That goes without saying. But we can't risk Calvin getting his mitts on you. He'd kill you."

I easily broke out of his grasp. "And he won't kill you?"

"Better me than you."

I narrowed my eyes. "That's a stupid thing to say. I can't lose you anymore than you can lose me."

"Quint, how many of them are there?" Ashton asked, breaking the tension rising between Mateo and me.

Quint folded his arms and leaned against a wall. "From what I can tell, there's about a dozen Unseelie and Dark Demons, in addition to Velkan and the demon wolves."

"Do you think there are more inside the witch's cabin?" Ashton asked.

Quint shrugged. "Maybe, but I don't know."

"I don't even see how they got inside. Last time we were here, the only ones who could get in were Hades and Salem." Frustration flared in his eyes and voice.

Mateo sighed and got a faraway look in his eyes. "Calvin could have forced Hayley to lift the spell. Pain can be very persuasive."

I shuddered at the thought of what Hayley might have endured.

"You were talking about a diversion," Quint said. "What kind of a diversion did you have in mind?"

I stared at Hades and broke out in a grin. "What if it was this little guy here that scared the pants off of them?"

Hades met my gaze and twitched his tail, as if he understood me.

Mateo frowned. "Hades? They might conclude that King Gunnar was attacking them. I'm not sure that's a good idea."

I searched his eyes. "But that's the whole point. That's the diversion, don't you see? Hades will lure them out."

"Maybe. But Hades doesn't go by himself," Quint said.

"You?" Ashton asked.

"Why not? Sometimes people mistake my bat for Anton's."

I gave him an incredulous look. "You want to drag Anton into this? He said he didn't want to get involved because it would be considered an act of war."

"Oh, what different does it make," Quint said angrily. "Using Hades will be the same thing."

I wasn't sure I agreed with that, but I didn't want Mateo to sacrifice himself either.

Mateo sat on one of the mats. "Tell me about these patrols."

"They're pretty regular. Every hour on the hour. I'm surprised that they didn't see you."

Mateo's eyes darkened. "How do you know they didn't?"

"Wait." Ashton looked at us. "Even if the patrols didn't spot us, can't the demon wolves smell Salem?"

"Of course they can," I said miserably. "I'm sure Velkan knows I'm here. He has to."

"Then we're going to have to fight our way in," Remi said. "I know you don't want to do this, Salem, but you're going to have use that damned spell. We'll cover you as best we can."

"No!" Mateo's loud voice nearly shook the bunker to its core.

I sat next to him. "You had a good plan, but that would have only worked if Velkan didn't know I was here. He does. We have to get Hayley and Gloria out."

"It's a trap." He grabbed my hand and squeezed it tight. "You know it is."

"Maybe, but what choice do we have?" I gave him a smirk. "You didn't think your new queen would be hiding in the shadows, did you?"

"No, but I don't want you to expose yourself to more danger than necessary, either. You remember what Queen Gwendoline said. This spell will drain your power. You'll be super vulnerable."

"Then when I do it, you must all cover me. Hades and I can't take all of them down by ourselves."

Hades snarled.

I knelt in front of him and rubbed his cheeks. "I know you're brave, little guy, but unfortunately, we're not a two-man army." I rested my forehead on his. "We need the whole team to do this."

He answered me by licking my face, breaking the tension and making me laugh.

"Fine. When should we execute this fantastic plan?" Mateo mumbled.

I glared. "You don't have to be such a grump about it."

Quint rubbed his cheek thoughtfully. "If they know we're here, I think they'll attack at dawn."

"Then we go now." I stood. "We need the element of surprise on our side." I got the *Book of Goody* out of the bag. It trembled in my arms. "We can't let Calvin get his hands on this."

Remi followed me. "Do you want to lock it in the store room, as I call it?"

"Yes, I do."

The book trembled again.

Don't leave me

But this time I ignored it.

"I'll be back," I whispered to it as I sat it on top of a counter.

Remi frowned. "Who are you talking to?"

"No one. Sorry." I didn't want to explain that the book and I talked sometimes, and right now it was scared.

Because it wasn't the only one trembling. I was too.

I put on my I'm-not-scared-of-anything face when I returned to the bunker, but my heart began to race faster and faster. One look at Mateo told him I was scared shitless, but that didn't matter. We had to get the two women and the Rose Box.

And the only way to do it was for me to perform the *Isois* spell that would allow all of us to get inside the witch's cabin.

"The smart thing would be to go at dawn," Mateo murmured.

I clasped his arm. "But don't you think they'll be expecting that?"

Mateo sighed. "Then we go tonight at midnight. It will give us a little time to rest first."

An uneasy feeling sunk in my gut. "Not now? The demon wolves can track me. They could come here."

"It's a chance we'll have to take," he said. "Our team is exhausted. We need to rest and be at full strength before we attack."

I wanted to argue but then I saw the tightness around my team's eyes and the dark circles underneath them . We'd trekked a hundred miles.

"Fine. At midnight."

We each selected a mat and stretched out on the ground. Remi had blankets in the store room that she doled out to everyone. I curled up next to Mateo and he wrapped his arm around my waist, holding me close. I didn't think I'd be able to sleep but my tired limbs and the lull of his heartbeat soon had me in dreamland...

I n my wolf form, I was walking alone through the forest to the witch's cabin. My paws crunched on the crisp snow. The full moon played hide and seek between the clouds, making the woods even more mysterious.

I came out of the woods and looked at the moonlight glistening off the black, still water. The boulder was just as I remembered it last time. It seemed to be just a large rock covered in a blanket of snow, but I knew better.

I slowly approached the boulder and sniffed. I wasn't the only wolf here, but the scent wasn't of my wolf pack. I had encountered it before. It was the demon wolves. They were close by, perhaps in the cabin waiting for me.

Only one way to find out. I jumped off the rock and just like last time, it magically appeared the minute my paws hit the stairs that led into the cabin. The door was open and I cautiously went inside.

Fear settled in my gut. My ears flattened and I let out a low, menacing growl.

Velkan and the demon wolves were waiting for me.

He flashed me an evil smile. His red eyes glowed. "Welcome. Soon your team will be dead. And you'll be our prisoner."

Snarling, I leapt toward him, but something hit me in the flank, stunning me—

I woke with a start and sat bolt upright. I was sweating profusely and my heart threatened to explode. I couldn't even breathe. My team was fast asleep, snoring softly. Had a spell been cast over them?

I sat in bed, rocking back and forth. What if Velkan was right? What if my entire team was killed? I couldn't live with that.

I wriggled out from Mateo's protective arm and then kissed him gently on his rugged chest. "I love you too much to watch you die," I breathed, softly so as not to wake him.

Hades raised his head, watching me intently. I wanted to tell him no, but he would growl and snarl, waking everyone else up. I couldn't have that.

I tilted my head toward the door that led outside. Terror gripped me tightly, nearly choking me, but I wouldn't let any of them be killed.

Take me with you, the *Book of Goody* called.

I gasped.

Shitshitshitshitshit

I wasn't sure if I should or not.

You'll need me. I can help you with the demon wolves.

Hades nudged my leg as if he could hear the voice too. That settled it.

I quietly slipped into the secret room that Remi had left open and grabbed the book. I hurried up the stairs and slipped out the door, with Hades right behind me.

I knelt next to him. "Listen, if something happens..." I lifted the book. "You take this and leave me. Go back to the others. Do you understand?"

He tipped his head back and forth. I wasn't sure if he understood, but it was a chance I had to take.

A tremor of fear went through me. Outside, it looked exactly like it had in my dream. Clouds slid past the moon like large birds of prey. The snow seemed brighter with the full moon shining on it. Through the dense woods, I couldn't make out any movement.

I inhaled and exhaled deeply, taking in sweet pine, but didn't detect any other wolves' or other supernaturals' scents.

Hades looked up with me with his golden eyes and I smiled. I was glad he was coming with me. I tucked the book underneath my arm. "Come on, boy. They're waiting for us. Let's not disappoint them."

18

Hades didn't take off, staying instead on the ground with me. We slowly made our way through the forest, stopping, listening, smelling. Nothing was amiss.

Or was it?

The voice had said it could help me with the demon wolves, so that meant there was a spell in it that would work against them. I hope I hadn't made a giant mistake.

I spread my palm over the leatherbound book again and closed my eyes.

Demon wolves. Show me how.

The familiar tingling sensation fluttered through me, spreading warmth within me like Mateo's touch. I opened my eyes and a breeze floated around me. The book's pages flipped slowly—thoughtfully, or was it afraid?—and stopped on *Morphello Refulsi*, a spell that apparently broke an Unseelie's dark magic. I groaned. This was worse than the *Isosi* spell that I had used to counter a witch's incantation. If I cast the *Morphello Refulsi* spell, the introduction explained, I couldn't use any other magic for at least twenty-four hours, or I would run the risk of killing myself.

And the worst part was, I would have to use the spell on each wolf individually, not all at once. It could take days.

"Fucking great," I muttered under my breath.

Hades stopped abruptly and looked at me with uneasiness.

Smiling, I rubbed his mane. "Sorry, buddy. Didn't mean to alarm you, but this is going to be harder than I thought."

Snap Snap Snap

My heart stopped.

We weren't alone.

I slowly stood and hid the book underneath my coat.

Crunch Crunch Crunch

I held my breath, waiting to be ambushed. Strangely, Hades didn't growl. In fact, he wagged his tail.

A tall, dark figure moved quickly through the trees toward us. "Salem?" an angry voice whispered.

Dammit! It was Mateo.

He came up alongside me and clasped my arm tightly. "Did you really think you could escape me?"

I stared into his furious eyes. "I didn't...I didn't want you to be killed."

"Salem, any of us could be killed, even you, especially if you're planning on taking on Calvin and his whole damned army single-handedly."

"Don't be mad. I had another dream..."

"What dream?"

I quickly told him.

Something flapped overhead and a huge bat swooped down, then changed into Quint. He folded his arms and stared at me accusingly. "Trying to go somewhere without us?"

Two wolves came up to, snarling—Remi's red one and Ashton's gray one.

"Okay, okay, I get it. I shouldn't have gone without you. Let me tell you why."

Like I had with Mateo, I caught them up to speed on what was happening.

When I finished, I couldn't stop the stupid tears from coming. "I didn't...I didn't want..."

Mateo took me in his arms. "I know, babe. I know. But you can't do this alone. None of us can. Calvin's too strong."

"And we are too," the magical voice from the *Book of Goody* said. *"Especially you."*

"Mateo," Quint said softly. "The only way this is going to work is if Salem uses the spell allowing all of us into the witch's cabin."

"I know." He unraveled from me and rested his forehead on me. "You stay close to me and Hades, understand? No matter what happens. Promise me."

I nodded.

Mateo stepped in front of me. "Let's go." He glanced over his shoulder. "Follow me–single file."

With each step, the cabin got closer and closer and all I could think about was my dream. Goosebumps broke out all over me as a feeling of dread and despair sank deeper and deeper into my gut. Had that been a warning? A premonition of the future? Or was Velkan just messing with me?

Mateo led us to the black, still lake that I had seen in my dream. The clouds floated around the moon and then shielded her, as if they didn't want her to see what would happen next. I swear the air crackled with tension.

This was it. We were going into battle, ready or not.

Mateo turned and looked at me. "Are you sure about this?"

"Unless you want me to go inside with just Hades."

"You know I don't."

I made a move to go past him and he grabbed me, pulling me against his chest. He brought his lips down on mine and kissed me brutally, as if this was the last time he'd taste me. I clung to his shoulders and kissed him back just as furiously. I melted into his arms and chest, my fingers clawing his hair. Our frantic hearts beat as one and love swelled inside my chest, threatening to burst it open.

He finally released me, panting as hard as I was, and cupped my face. "I love you."

"Me too." God, why couldn't I tell him how I felt in so many words? What the hell was wrong with me? He was my mate and was everything to me, and I still hadn't told him I loved him. Something always made me hold back.

Without another word, I headed toward the boulder, my pack following me, ready to lunge inside. I glanced over my shoulder and for half a breath, I thought about leaping into the cabin alone.

Then everything happened so fast and all at once that I didn't even get a chance to utter the spell.

Hades released a low, warning growl and flipped out his wings.

His eyes turned gold.

A pack of wolves rushed out from behind the boulder. Or had it been from the witch's cabin? There had to be at least twenty of them.

Crap, twenty against six.

"Salem, shift!" someone yelled. I wasn't sure who it was, but it might have been Mateo. He didn't have to tell me twice.

I took out the *Book of Goody* and looked at Hades who was standing in front of me.

"Hades, take this to safety."

He looked over his shoulder, confused, but he grabbed the book in his mouth and took off just as a wolf rushed me.

I ran, tearing off my coat and then my sweater. Wonder Woman adrenaline pumped through me, slamming through every muscle, making me move, move, MOVE. My wolf was already clawing inside me, trying to reach the surface. She wanted out. She wanted to fight. She wanted to tear this bastard apart.

And she wouldn't be denied.

Faster than I thought possible, I shifted into my beautiful wolf, tearing through my jeans and boots.

I whipped around to face my attacker. I was twice as big as him and three times as angry. He halted and fear flashed in his eyes, and he turned to retreat, but he wasn't fast enough.

Snarling and growling, I lunged and bit his throat open, ripping and tearing, tasting his blood.

Yelp Yelp Yelllp

The bastard whimpered one more time and then went limp in my mouth. I tossed him aside. His body slammed into a tree and he didn't get up.

Ashton and Mateo were fighting together, taking down wolves one by one. Quint's eyes were bright red. He grabbed a squirming wolf, sinking his fangs deep into his neck.

Hades returned and exhaled a stream of fire, setting three wolves alight. I inhaled the smell of burnt fur and scorched flesh. Flames flickered on the wolves' backs, sending smoke swirling in the air, making my eyes water. The three beasts howled as they rolled on the ground, trying to extinguish the flames.

Two other wolves had Remi cornered. Blood dripped down the side of her throat.

Grrrrrr

Rage pulsed through me, sending power through me like a bulldozer, knocking down all my fear, and without hesitation I smashed into the first wolf, knocking him into the second. My ears flattened, my hackles bristling, I stood in front of Remi, daring them to attack me.

Stupidly, they did.

They lunged at the same time, but I was ready for them. I swatted the first one with my paw, sending him flying onto his side. The other bit my flank but I kicked him hard, easily breaking free of his sharp teeth.

He yelped as blood dripped from his mouth as if he had bitten his tongue.

"Hello, Salem," a cruel voice said.

Pulling back my upper lip and snarling, I turned my head and froze.

Velkan and the demon wolves had cut me and Remi off from the rest of the team. Death reflected in their eyes. I blocked Remi from coming forward. She'd never survive this attack. Hell, I didn't know if I would.

Mateo's black wolf was fighting desperately to get here, tossing his enemies to the side, a wolf on a mission.

Velkan unleashed his sword. "You've made a serious mistake, Princess. You will come with me, or my demon wolves will rip your aunt to pieces."

Hades landed next to me and roared.

"We have something special for you." Something moved in the trees like a black cloud.

He pointed his sword. "That, my dear Princess, is the Darkness from the Elder Dimension."

I vaguely remembered reading something about the Darkness. It was some kind of monster that even Raven hesitated to fight. I shivered.

Crap, we were screwed.

That thing could destroy my whole pack. There was only one thing to do. These bastards wanted me, not my team.

I nipped at one of the demon wolves, who snarled. I jumped over Hades and bolted back into the forest with the demon wolves right on my tail, leading them farther and farther away from my team. I knew Hades would protect Remi. Velkan wouldn't be able to get near her.

The demon wolves chased me. They were damned fast. A few more quick steps and they would have me, but I had a surprise for them. I leapt over a boulder and shifted, just as they surrounded me.

Naked and shivering, I fixed my gaze on the wolf closest to me. Hoping this would work, I said in a loud voice, *"Morphello Refulsi."*

It was as if something took over my body. My arms stretched

out and I shook violently as if I was going into convulsions. My teeth chattered uncontrollably even as hot tingling sensations surged through me and I felt like I'd just been struck by lightning. My hair flew around my face. Black, white, and pink colors temporarily blinded my vision.

Yelp Yelp

My vision cleared and I watched helplessly as the demon wolf I had directed the spell to lifted off the ground. A pink aura with white stars swirled around the beast and suddenly a dark mass spewed from its mouth.

The black mass jetted through me like a sharp knife, cutting into my flesh. I screamed. It was cold and evil, squeezing my insides tighter and tighter and tighter. Black spots floated in front of my eyes and I couldn't exhale.

Pop Pop

One, then two, ribs cracked.

Then suddenly it all stopped.

I tilted head my back and the last thing I saw was a dark mass covering the stars. Then it descended on me like a cold, icy fog.

Someone yelled, "Salem, where are you?"

It was Mateo. I wanted to answer him, but I was paralyzed by the black fog. It lifted me higher and higher off the snow-covered ground. Terror that this thing was going to drop me like a sack of potatoes seized me, but then it rushed across the treetops and over the mountain like a shooting black star with me in its clutches.

I struggled but I couldn't even move my little finger. It was as if I was stuck to fly paper. Through my hair plastered to my face, I could see where it was taking me.

All hope flowed from me. I could feel the blood on my face drain into my churning gut. My mouth turned dry and my heart stilled. Warning bells rang in my head, you're dead, you're dead.

The Darkness was taking me to Iredale Palace.

And I knew I would never make it out of there alive.

redale Palace was just as ominous tonight as it was the last time I saw it. The gray stone castle rivaled the mountains in its majesty—he twelve-foot-thick walls had to be at least forty feet tall, the sentry walks at least a mile long. Armed guards patrolled the walkway, not with guns, since bullets were useless against supernatural beings, but with swords, crossbows, and bows and arrows.

The moon backlit the palace, and the silhouette of its ramparts, towers, and spires sent cold dread to every bone in my body. Flickering torches blazed in the iron crescents on either side of the barbican towers, the only lights that could I see trapped as I was in the belly of the Darkness. Once inside, it would be difficult for my pack to rescue me. I was as good as dead.

My captor descended toward the palace, ramping up my fear.

Within the fortress, there was a snow-covered bailey and keep that was the largest tower and the most heavily fortified. Calvin's sleeping quarters were at the very top and his balcony looked over the courtyard so he could see for miles around. A lone figure stood there now, dressed in a thick fur coat. That had to be Calvin. The Darkness dropped me to the ground, stark naked. The wind was knocked out of me and pain pulsed inside me. I got up on my shaky legs and promptly fell down again.

Guards rushed toward me, swords drawn, their excited voices chilling my bones.

"Get the bitch!"

"Don't let her shift."

Seize her."

I called on my wolf but she had disappeared entirely. God, what had happened to her? I pounded my fists and kicked at the first guard who seized me, but he smacked me across the cheek. Pain exploded in my face and blood rolled down onto my lips.

He hauled me to my feet. "Someone wants to see you."

I wanted to fight but using that spell had drained me and I was as a weak as a dandelion puff blowing in the wind.

He twisted my arm behind my back and dragged me across the courtyard. Guards surrounded us and accompanied me across the snowy courtyard. The bitter cold froze my feet and sharp rocks cut into my heels, but the bastard didn't slow down.

"Please, I can't keep up."

"Shut up." He dragged me to a cement stairwell that wound down to a heavy metal door.

Another guard came and unlocked it.

I gasped. It was a cold, filthy dungeon. He dragged me to an empty cell and tossed me in. I shivered uncontrollably. There wasn't even as much as a blanket. I tried to shift but nothing happened. Disappointment almost reduced me to tears. Where was my wolf when I needed her? What had that damned spell done to me? I didn't even know if it had worked. The Darkness had seized me before I had a chance to find out.

Heavy footsteps crossed the floor. "Put this on." Someone threw me an oversized gray top and a pair of pants that reminded me of scrubs. "Get dressed so you're decent before the king comes down here."

Shit, the king? I was going to meet my uncle face to face? This fucking sucked. What had I been thinking? It wasn't supposed to have gone this way.

My belly quivered and my hands shook as I put on the outfit. The thin material did nothing to keep out the cold. I almost hoped I froze to death before I met my uncle. There was a rolled-up mattress on a rusted cot. I unrolled it and sat down, wrapping my arms around my waist, shivering.

Something caught my eye in the next cell and I skidded across the mattress. "Who's there?"

Someone clasped the bars and pressed their face against them. No. It couldn't be. Same blue gown, same blond hair, same haunted look.

Gloria.

"Salem? Is that you? Is Ashton safe?"

"I...I...d-don't know." I could barely get the words out because my teeth were chattering so badly. "I thought...I th-thought y-y-you were in the witch's c-ca-cabin."

She shook her head. "No. None of us were."

Everything went still and I could feel the blood drain from my face. "Wh-wha-at? But I saw it in a v-v-v-ision."

"Calvin forced Hayley to cast a spell. He was leading you into a trap."

"But-but...I used a sp-sp-spell of my own."

Soft footsteps approached us.

"Oh, no...he's...he's coming."

Gloria immediately retreated and disappeared into a corner.

Something inside me wouldn't let me cower in the same way. Showing fear had never been an option in foster care and it wouldn't be an option now.

The same man I had seen standing on the balcony wearing the fur coat stood in front of me now. He had black hair and deep blue eyes like my father, but his expression was cruel and his face was too narrow.

He flashed his gaze over me. "So, you're my brother's daughter

141

who's after my crown." His voice crushed all of my fear. The only thing I wanted to do was scratch his eyes out.

I lifted my head up high. "You mean the one you murdered to steal?"

He gave me a sinister smile that curdled my blood. "You'll lose that tone once I'm done with you, my dear."

I tried to hold my chin steady, but my defiance deflated. Images of what he had done to Ashton and Mateo flashed in my mind and I couldn't hold back a shudder.

Triumph flared in his cold eyes. "There will be time to teach you a lesson in humility later." He flicked up his collar. "But it's far too chilly in here to do anything now. Tomorrow will be fine." He bowed slightly. "I'll leave you with your thoughts."

He put his hands behind his back and strolled past my cell. Not once did even glance at Gloria who was softly crying.

The door shut. He was gone.

I hurried over to the bars. "Gloria, wh-where's Hayley?" God, I was sick of my teeth chattering and shivering like this.

She didn't even look at me and refused to speak.

"Gloria, pl-please, answer me."

She merely shook her head and whimpered.

The poor girl was frightened out of her mind. I couldn't imagine what Calvin had done to her—or what he was going to do to me tomorrow. Tears of frustration blurred my vision. I dropped my arms and sat back on my cot.

Everything snowballed inside me. The battle, the spells, and the capture. I curled up into a tight ball on the cot, thinking of my team. More tears slid down onto the bare cot. Had they made it out alive? What happened to the demon wolf had I used the spell on? Was it still under Velkan's control? If my vision was wrong, maybe that had been too.

My thoughts weren't enough to keep me awake and I fell into an exhausted sleep, where not even dreams could disturb me.

All too soon, someone roughly pulled me off the cot. "Get up."

I blinked, not sure what was happening. I stumbled to my feet, stubbing my big toe on the bar door as I did so. I cried out.

"Shut up, you dumb bitch." The guard dragged me past the other cells. Some had prisoners. Others were empty. The prisoners all looked the same, wearing the same thin pajamas and appearing more dead than alive with their sunken eyes, disheveled hair, and clothes hanging off their emaciated bodies. I wondered if I would look like them soon, or if I would even live that long.

The next thing I knew I was being dragged up the stairs and thrown into a small room that more closely resembled a closet. The guard put his hand over my mouth: my first thought was that he was going to rape me. My thundering heart sent power to my tired limbs, but it wasn't enough. I struggled, hitting and kicking him, but I far too weak to fight back.

He put a finger to his lips. "Shhh, I'm not going to hurt you. I'm Edward Wayland. I'm a friend of Mateo's."

I immediately stilled, panting, and stared into his blue eyes, not sure I could trust him, especially after he dragged me through the dungeon like a bag of trash.

His white hair dangled in front of my eyes. "I'm going to lower my hand now." He moved his palm away from my mouth and I was tempted to bite it. "Will you promise not to scream?"

I narrowed my eyes. "Why the hell should I trust you, asshole?"

He placed his hands on either side of my face. "Because I'm the only chance you have of getting out of her alive, Princess."

I lifted up my chin, not buying anything he was saying. This was probably one of Calvin's new ways to torture someone.

"Edward?" Some called from outside the door.

"Dammit," he mumbled. He grabbed my wrist hard and tossed me roughly out of the closet. "Try that again, Princess, and you're dead."

I rubbed my throbbing wrist, glad I had trusted my instincts not to trust this douchebag.

"Was she giving you a hard time, Wayland?"

Edward tilted his head and snickered. "She tried to escape and got trapped in the closet."

The other guard shook his head. "What a dumb bitch."

I glared. "Quit calling me that."

The guard crowded me against the wall. "I'll call you whatever I want, Princess." He squeezed my breast hard. "The king said once he was done with you, we could have some fun with you."

I gritted my teeth. "Get. Off. Me."

Edward pulled the creep off me. "Bill, leave her alone. You know the king doesn't like to be kept waiting."

Bill stepped away and straightened his shirt. "Yeah, sure." I could detect fear in his voice. That was the one good thing about my uncle—he at least instilled fear into would-be rapists.

He wasn't the only one.

I slapped Bill as hard as I could across the face, leaving a hand print on his cheek. "Don't ever touch me again."

"You bitch." He lunged for me, his fist closed.

Edward grabbed his arms, pinning them behind them. "Leave her be, dude. It's not worth it."

Bill got loose and held up one finger. "You ever touch me again. You'll live to regret it."

I opened my mouth to spit a sharp retort but Edward shook his head and gave me a don't-push-your-luck look. Edward clasped my arm and led me down a hallway. My bare feet stuck to the hardwood floor and I wished I at least had some slippers or could shift into my wolf.

Two men were guarding double doors. One of them opened a door for us that led into what I could only describe as a board room, with bookcases and a long rectangular wooden table with matching wooden chairs with red velvet seat cushions. This room had wall to wall red carpet and my feet sank deep into warmth for the first time. My uncle sat at the head of the long table and was writing something on a piece a paper. He didn't even look up. Such a pompous ass.

He laid down his pen and folded his hands on the paper. "Ah, Salem. I hope you had a pleasant night."

I gave him a haughty glare, refusing to play his stupid little game.

He motioned to the chair next to him. "Please, sit down."

I curled my toes into the carpet and crossed my arms across my chest.

"Bill, would you please help Salem to sit down?"

"With pleasure." He wrapped his fingers in my hair, yanking hard, and pulled out the chair. "Sit."

That hurt like hell. I blinked away the tears and kept my hands pinned to my side to keep from rubbing the back of my neck. Edward didn't make the slightest move to help me. Yeah, I can really trust you, buddy.

"Now, Salem," my uncle began. "It has come to my attention that you possess a book that I've been searching for—the *Book of Goody*."

I stared at him, hoping my face looked as impassive as Mateo's when he was hiding his feelings.

Calvin didn't seem the least put out. "Two can play that same game, Salem. I know how to get a reaction from you." He rubbed his lower lip. "I just heard from Velkan" —fear fluttered in my gut — "and he reported that your team is dead."

My face crumpled and my throat collapsed. I couldn't breathe and I couldn't hold back the tears that shook me to my very core. His words cut through my chest, slicing my ribs, slashing my heart into tiny pieces. I wanted to be strong like my wolf, like Mateo, but once again, my uncle had taken everything away that I loved and my strength with it.

My wolf howled in anguish. I couldn't hold back her mournful song.

Aaaaaaaaooo Aaaaaaooo Aaaaaaooo

She was as devastated as I was. It was an agony I had never known—chilling, tingling, prickling like cold tendrils wrapping around my ankles, crushing my breath, and creeping up my spine to the back of my neck until I tilted my head back and released another searing howl.

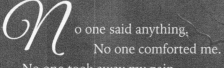o one said anything.
    No one comforted me.
No one took away my pain.

I was alone. Hades was gone. Remi was gone. Ashton was gone. Quint was gone.

Mateo…I couldn't even think it…Mateo was gone, too.

Calvin had fucking killed my mate and I had never told Mateo that I loved him. I nearly choked on my own bitterness. He died not knowing I loved him.

Something burst inside me and I lunged for my uncle, snarling, trying to scratch his cheeks with my fingernails. I wanted blood. I wanted to hurt him just as much as he had me.

"I'm going to fucking kill you." I swiped my hand, scratching his cruel face.

He jerked back. "How dare you touch me," he said icily.

I climbed up on the table, ready to do much worse than that.

Edward and Bill grabbed my arms and yanked me off the table.

"Shit, this girl's strong," Bill groaned.

He hadn't seen anything yet. My wolf had awakened and she was coming to the surface.

Calvin looked at the smeared blood on his palm. "You'll pay for hurting me, Salem."

"Like I give a shit."

He glared. "Ah, but you will. You'll die, just like your wretched teammates died."

I pulled on my arms, but it was as if they were locked in steel traps. "You'll regret killing my team." I wanted to see fear in his eyes. "King Gunnar will retaliate if you killed Hades."

"I wouldn't worry about that." Calving got out of his chair and uneasiness flashed in his eyes, but then a devious smile flashed across his face that chilled my blood. "King Gunnar won't be a king much longer."

"What?" I struggled with my captors. If I got loose, every single one of them would be dead.

Calvin edged away from me. "Chain her up next to Hayley."

I pulled and yanked on my arms and kicked my feet. My wolf was almost here—

Then someone clocked me hard in the back of my skull and all went blank.

I woke to excruciating pain in the back of my head and my stomach swished uneasily. I was stuffed in a tiny cage that could barely hold me. My wrists and ankles were manacled. I couldn't move an inch.

"He's really pissed at you," someone said softly.

"Well, so am I." I looked up to see Hayley looking at me with sorrowful eyes. She was in a small cell, too, but it was ten times bigger than mine.

I gazed in horror at the chains dangling from the wall, the rack, the breaking wheel, the iron maiden—oh, crap. I knew where I was.

"I am in his secret room, aren't I?"

"Yeah. You're here to join the fun." She sighed. "He wants that spell book, Salem, and he'll do anything to get it."

"But why am I in such a small cage? Does he think I'm a cocker spaniel?"

"He plans to roast you alive over a fire. A small cage is easier to transport." Her words slashed through me, slicing into my heart, my lungs, and my soul.

"He would do that?"

She nodded. "It's very effective." She lowered her head. "The balls of my feet and my palms will be scarred for life."

I gasped. "Oh, my god, Hayley. That's horrible."

She looked at me and gave me a warm smile. "I know. That's why I can't let the same thing happen to you."

I frowned, trying to wrap my brain around her statement. "What? Why would you do that?"

"Because you're the missing princess, the rightful heir. Calvin has to be stopped. He's getting more and more evil. Look at me. Look what he's done to his own daughter."

She smiled again. "If I help you get out, you need to promise me one thing."

Was I going to have to give her my first-born child? I looked at her warily. "Sure. Anything...I guess..."

She looked at me with pleading puppy dog eyes. "Take Gloria with you. She won't last much longer in here."

I studied her, wishing I could read minds. "Why do you want to save Gloria?"

She looked sad and thoughtful. "I've been here a long, long time, Salem. I don't have many friends."

I gave her a tight smile. "So, she's your friend?"

Hayley nodded. "Hard to believe, but true. I can't let her die or be tortured any longer. Will you promise me you'll get her out of here? These are Unseelie chains. I can't—"

Not again.

"I can try, Haley, but it drains my power. To be honest, I tried breaking the spell on one of the demon wolves and I'm not even sure it worked. Even if did, it doesn't matter." My voice cracked and my lower lip trembled.

"What do you mean?"

"Calvin said that my team is all…" I couldn't say the word. If I said it, it made it real.

"Dead?"

I bit my lip and nodded, trying to stay in control, but my pain was bubbling up in my throat. I couldn't control it.

Aaaaaaaooo

I released another long, mournful howl and hung my head in utter defeat.

"Salem, listen to me. Shhh." She looked toward the door and back to me frantically. "You've got to get control of yourself. They'll hear you."

"I have no one now, Hayley. Don't you get it?" My voice shook with rage and sorrow. It was the damned foster care system all over again.

"Snap out of it, Salem. Your team will have died for nothing if you give up. Is that what you want?"

"No," I said miserably. "But how can I go on without them?"

"Because you're the lost princess. Your people are counting on it. What do you think living under your uncle's tyranny has been like for them?"

"An endless nightmare?"

"Yes. So what are you going to do about it?"

I paused, took a breath, then lifted my head up. "Take back my crown."

"Good." She smiled. "*Restora Honorius.*"

The chains fell from my wrists and ankles, and the lock on the door clicked open. I kicked it open and crawled out. The floor was cold and I crunched up my toes.

"Remember that spell," Hayley said. "It's the only way you can free Gloria."

I concentrated, not breathing, not talking, barely moving, hoping Calvin wouldn't burst through that door and cut me down.

I scanned the room, looking for a set of keys. "What about you, Hayley? You have to come with me."

"You know I can't. It's okay. He can't kill me, Salem. If he tries, because of my spell, he'll die the same way he kills me." Her voice was weary.

"But he can torture you," I said softly. "I can't leave you. This is the second time you've helped me. Please, let me help you in return."

"Don't worry, Salem. I'll survive. You must get out of here—take Gloria with you—and whatever you do, don't let Calvin get the *Book of Goody*." Her voice sounded confident, but I could see it in her eyes. Her facade was beginning to break and the fear behind it was slipping out. Calvin was definitely breaking her spirit.

"I won't. Thank you."

She lowered her voice. "There's one more thing."

I stilled, hoping it wasn't more bad news like Calvin had some hideous monster especially designed to eat me.

She looked around as if she was worried someone in here could be listening. "I need to tell you about the Rose Box and the key."

Goosebumps ran up my arms. "What about it?"

"I hid the key where no one can find it. Only my familiar can."

I frowned. "Your familiar?"

"Yes, Freedom. He's a bald eagle and he's been watching my place. He'll show you where the key is hidden. When you see a bald eagle near my home, say *Apericus Horrificus*. Freedom will recognize you and know you're a friend. He can understand us. Trust him."

The last thing I wanted to do was go back to her home where my team had died. What if their bodies had been left to rot where they were cut down? My mouth turned dry and my heart turned to dust. "Why can't you tell me where it is?"

"Because the walls have ears in this place. Go, now, before it's too late."

"Somehow I'll get you out of here." A thought hit me. "Why isn't Calvin here, especially since he wants that book so badly?"

"To tell you the truth, I don't know. The only thing that would keep him from torturing you is if Iredale Palace was under attack."

"Really? This place is a fortress. Why would he even be worried?"

"No one can bust through the walls of Iredale Palace. It's the portals that he's worried about it."

The portals. I remembered Ashton telling me about those.

"Calvin's worst fear is that there would be a secret coup to overthrow him from one of the other kingdoms launched via one of the portals," Haley continued. "However, he soon discovered that he couldn't destroy the one here. The only thing he could do was move it."

"So, where did he move it to?"

"The dungeon. However, if anyone comes through the portal, they are trapped in the dungeon and can't get out."

"What if an entire army comes through?"

"Unfortunately, he forced me to curse the cell and it will expand as needed." She gave me an apologetic smile. "I'm sorry. It sucks being his slave."

"I get it. Okay, say I wanted to use the portal, what would I say?"

Fear flashed in her eyes. "You can't do that. Don't even think it. The minute you walked into the cell, you'd be trapped."

"Gloria's in the dungeon, Hayley, and she's in pretty bad shape. I think she might have lost her mind. If I could get her to one of the other wolf kingdoms, they maybe could heal her. I don't know of other way to get her out of here. Do you?"

Hayley lowered her head. "Dammit." She looked at me with anguish in her eyes. "I don't. The spell's *Transerio Virtiseo*. You can try it, but..."

My brows furrowed. "Which cell is it?"

"You'll know it when you smell it. It has the most putrid stench."

Great. "Thank you."

"For what? I just might have signed yours and Gloria's death warrants."

"Maybe. Then again, I might surprise you and have some tricks up my sleeve." I gave her a confident smile, even though my knees were banging against each other.

"Good luck."

I held up a finger. "I have one last question."

"Yes?"

"Do you know if there is a plot to kill King Gunnar?"

Please say no Please say no Please say no

She sighed and leaned her head back. "He has many enemies, Salem. I'm afraid so."

"Then I've got to warn him."

"Well, you'd better hurry." She tilted her head toward the door that led to Calvin's bedroom. "Calvin could be coming in here any minute."

I didn't argue and hurried toward the door. I pressed my ear against the wood, listening, but the only thing I could hear was the pounding of my own heart. I glanced back at Hayley. She silently mouthed 'go'.

I took a deep breath and put my hand on the door. It was magically sealed, but I had opened it last time and I hoped the same luck would shine on me now. Tingling sensations fluttered in my chest and moved down my arm. Pink sparkles swirled around my fingers.

Click

I forced myself to turn the doorknob slowly and peek into Calvin's elaborate bedroom. His over-the-top luxury bedroom decorated with gold—I bet even the sheets on his canopy bed were gold—was empty.

Phew

I slipped into the bedroom and headed over to the door that led to the sitting room. Once again, I listened intently for any movement but heard nothing but my panting breath.

I opened the door to the sitting room. Empty. Lady luck was still smiling on me. I pressed my back against the wall and tried to still my breathing.

Calmdowncalmdowncalmdowncalmdown

I wished Mateo was here to help me, but I was on my own. Thinking about him revved up my grief but I shoved it down. There would be time to deal with my sorrow later, but not now. Not here.

I edged toward the door and grasped the door knob, slowly turning it and counting down.

One…Two…Three…

Inhaling and exhaling, I slowly peeked out. The hallway was clear but I could hear yelling, the thumping of feet, the growling and snarling.

I shut the door again. One tremor after another went through me, turning me into a shaking Chihuahua. Shit, what was I going to do?

Thinkthinkthinkthink

I couldn't stay in here and hide under my uncle's bed. I glanced at the French doors that led out to the balcony, wishing Raven and Hades were here or at least coming. Thinking of Hades brought tears to my eyes and made my heart sick.

Stop it

I shoved a shaking hand through my hair. WTF was I going to do?

I thought of Mateo and bit my lip. The one thing he wouldn't do was stand around with his thumb up his butt trying to figure out his next move.

I had to do something. I had to do something now or my ass was grass.

Once again, I opened the door. The heavy footsteps, snarls and growls were coming from farther down this hallway. Forcing my fear down, I slid out from behind the door and proceeded down the corridor, pressing close to the wall, wishing my wolf would make an appearance.

Each step I took, the shouts got louder, and then I heard screams as well—horrible, agonizing screams.

I froze, not sure what to do.

Then someone put their palm over my mouth, smothering my cries of frustration, and slipped their hand around my waist, pinning my arms to my side, slamming my back against their chest.

I inhaled the male scent. I knew who it was.

I was totally screwed.

21

My heart thundered in my chest, sending frustration and anger through me. Something else too—my wolf awakened. I could feel her. I released a low, warning growl.

"Don't scream. Don't move. If you do, they'll hear you."

It was Edward. Mr. Traitor.

My wolf ached to rip him to pieces.

He lowered his palm from my mouth and lessened the pressure around my arms.

Bad mistake, dude.

I elbowed him in the ribs as hard as I could.

He doubled over, holding his sides, hissing.

My wolf was about to break free and unbelievable strength pumped through me. I grabbed him by the neck and shoved him against the wall.

"What do you want?" I growled. My muscles bulged and my teeth sharpened.

He grabbed my arm. "Salem, wait…" He choked and sputtered. "Mateo—"

I gritted my teeth. My voice was a snarl. "What about him?"

"Damn it, why are you so strong?" He could barely get the words out.

"My wolf is about to break free." I flashed him an evil smile, revealing lots of teeth. "And then you'll be sorry."

Beads of sweat broke out across his lower lip. "Wait. Listen. Mateo told me to protect you."

"I don't need protecting." I tossed him on the floor. "Especially by you."

He put up his palms. "I know you're pissed, but I couldn't help you earlier. I couldn't betray the underground network. Too many lives are at stake." He was talking quickly, practically tripping over his words.

I cocked my eyebrow, waiting for him to hang himself some more. He was such a fucking liar.

"You don't understand, Salem. Bill's loyal to Calvin. I couldn't say or do anything."

More shouts echoed down the hallway. I couldn't waste time arguing with this dude.

"Yeah, I got that, but I trust you about as much as I trust him." I pressed my back against the wall and edged toward the angry voices, not that I wanted to, but I thought the door to the dungeon was located down there.

Edward immediately stepped in front of me and folded his arms. "Where are you going?"

I narrowed my eyes. "Why should I tell you?"

"Because I can help you."

"Oh, you mean like you did when Bill tried to rape me."

"I would never have allowed that. I did get him to stop, remember?" His defensive tone pissed me off.

"Why do you want to help me?"

He looked at me as if I had started speaking another language. "Seriously? Why do you think?" He rolled his eyes. "Because you're the missing princess. I want the crown to be restored to you as much as Mateo does."

"That's highly unlikely." I couldn't stop my voice from cracking.

"What's wrong?"

"Nothing." I refused to go down the road of grief with this dude. I was barely hanging on as it was.

He dropped his arms. "Okay, I get it. You don't trust me. But I have to tell you that this hallway is about to be crawling with Calvin's royal guard and I suggest we get the fuck out of here right the fuck now."

"We? As if."

A flicker of sadness flashed in his eyes but then it was gone. "Do you know your way around Iredale Palace, Princess?"

"I don't." I jammed an accusing finger into his chest. "But how do I know you're not leading us into a trap?"

"You don't. You just have to trust me. You ever heard of trust? I've to get you out of here. I owe Mateo."

Anger burned in my gut at his statement. At how he'd allowed Bill to practically rape me.

The howls and yells and heavy footsteps were getting closer.

"Salem." He looked over my head as if he was seeing at a ghost.

It wasn't a ghost. It was a swarm of shadows.

"Lead me to the dungeon."

He did a double take. "Excuse me?"

"Take me. Now."

He seized my arm. "Okay. Follow me."

God, I hoped I wasn't making a gigantic mistake. We ran down the hall, practically flying. He turned down another hallway that ended at a metal door.

Thud Thud Thud Thud

The angry footsteps kept time with the blood thumping through my temples. My wolf pushed at me, eager to take them on, but I shoved her back down.

Not now.

Not yet.

"This way." Someone yelled behind us.

"I can smell her." Someone else said and my gut tightened as I recognized Bill's foul voice.

CrapCrapCrapCrap

Edward opened a door that led to a spiral staircase filled with a disgusting stench that reminded me of rotting garbage. Flickering torches lit up the stained steps. Were the stains dried blood?

"Follow this down to the bottom. It will take you to another door that leads to the dungeon. I hope you know what you're doing. No one's ever escaped from that hellhole."

I narrowed my eyes. "You're not coming with me?"

"No, I have to hold them off and create a distraction. Good luck."

I didn't have a choice. I nodded and stepped inside the stairwell. He slammed the door behind me.

I held my breath and wished my pounding heart would shut up so I could listen for any footsteps or whispers, but it drowned everything else out. I got closer to the metal door but the only thing I could hear was muffled voices. I couldn't make out the words, and I sure wasn't going to stick around to find out.

I descended the stairs as quietly as possible. Slimy liquid dripped down the walls and pooled at the bottom of the stairs. I wrinkled my nose at the stench. God, it was awful.

Worse, was there was no railing, so I couldn't hold on to anything to make sure I didn't slip on that stuff. Cold air blew around me, sending the stench even more into my nostrils, making me feel dirty. I forced myself to move, even though I had never felt so alone and my heavy heart just wanted to wallow in misery.

Tears slipped down my cheeks as I went down the steps and hate swelled in my gut. All I wanted to do was tear this place down piece by piece and destroy all of Calvin's dreams. It wasn't enough just to kill him. I wanted him to suffer like he had made everyone else suffer.

It was a long freaking stairwell. The deeper I went the colder and filthier it got—mold, spider webs, lichen clinging to the walls, and, oh God, the smell. It just got worse and worse.

At last I reached the bottom of the stairwell and came face to face with a metal door. Two torches were on either side of it. Time to find out if Edward was true to his word. If he was, this would lead into the dungeon.

I twisted the doorknob and it clicked open.

You can do this. I whispered the words over and over in my mind. My team—Mateo—would want me to go on.

I pulled on the door and was back in the dungeon where I had started from in the first place. Hmm, Edward had been telling the truth. I wouldn't forget that.

The dungeon had that same musty smell, that same miserable light, and that same feeling of despair as when I was imprisoned here. The place was draped in fear like a scratchy blanket, making my spirit itch. I waited for my eyes to adjust to the darkness before I took another step.

Not all the cells were full, but the ones that were, I could sense the hopelessness. God, how could I rescue Gloria and leave the others behind? If I could open that damned portal for two people, all of us should be able to get through. Shouldn't we? I had to try.

I slowly moved down the corridor between the cells. The occupants all had the same vacant look Gloria had. Some of them I couldn't even tell if they were male or female. They'd just be left down here to rot.

Enough. They were my people and I wouldn't leave them here, dying in a pool of despair.

I spread my arms wide and in a loud voice, I said, "*Restora Honorius.*" Tingling sensations spread through me and pink sparkles flew from my fingertips. The sparkles swirled in and out of the cells. Loud clicks sounded one by one as then the doors slowly creaked open.

None of the poor occupants moved, as if afraid it was a trick.

"I am Salem Willis, daughter of King Andre and Queen Libby. I am the missing Wolf Princess. I have come to set you free. All of you, follow me." My strong voice hid the fear rippling through me. I had to be brave for my people.

Some of the sad sacks shuffled out of the cells like zombies. God, they weren't actually monsters, were they?

"Salem?" One of the ragtag crowd stepped closer. Tangled blond hair, blue stained gown, dirt smeared on their face.

I smiled. "Gloria."

"What are you doing here?" Her voice was barely a whisper.

"I'm here to rescue you."

"There's no way out of here," a hollow male voice whispered. "Except to the gallows with a hood over your head."

I sniffed and caught the grossest, foulest smell imaginable. It made me think of what a rotting corpse must smell like. Immediately my team snapped into my mind and I could see flies buzzing around their dead bodies.

NoNoNoNoNo

Stop. Don't think about it.

I braced my shoulders. "You're wrong. Come with me."

I headed toward the stench.

"No one goes back there," Gloria whispered. "That cell is cursed."

I glanced over my shoulder at her and all the other prisoners' blank faces. "You have to, if you want to escape."

God, I hoped I was telling the truth.

I stopped in front of the cell and almost jumped back to join the others. I could feel the dark magic as if it was something alive, huddling in the corner, staring at me. Goosebumps broke out on my shivering skin. Huge, fat spiders sat in their webs and I could feel their eyes on me. Rats scurried around the floor, then suddenly stopped and stared at me as if daring me to enter the cell. I knew if I did, the spiders and rats would attack me.

Fear burned inside me like a fire, incinerating my courage, but I wasn't going to let Calvin win. I owed it to my team.

Once again, I spread out my arms wide, drawing on my power. This time after the tingling sensations began to ripple through me, an invisible force pushed me back, making me stumble. Icy fingers gripped my neck, sending shivers of fear through me.

What the hell

I broke away and rubbed my stinging neck. Wetness coated my hand and it came away red. Whatever that invisible force had been, it had scratched me. This wasn't going to be easy.

I took a deep breath, spread my legs shoulder width apart, and narrowed my eyes.

Then I lifted my chin in absolute defiance. *"Morphello Refulsi."*

Something shrieked inside the cage. Spiders and rats disappeared one by one, taking the miserable stench with them.

All my energy slowly dissolved like a fizzing Alka-Seltzer tablet. I collapsed onto my knees, barely able to breathe.

Someone rushed over to me.

"Salem, what did you do?"

It took everything I had to look into Gloria's wide, frightened eyes.

Heavy steps thundered toward us.

"Princess, they're coming." A woman's terrified voice spurred me on.

"Transerio Viritiseo." My voice was the tiniest squeak.

"Oh my God, look!" Gloria hugged me. "The portal. It's open."

A blue spinning circle had formed in the middle of the cell, growing and growing.

I had done it. My people were free. They could get out.

Angry voices were behind the door.

"Go. Go, all of you, quickly," I whispered.

"No, I won't leave you." Then Gloria's voice dropped away as if she had fallen into a deep well.

My eyes fluttered shut and I couldn't move. Movement and stampeding footsteps were all around me.

Something sharp tugged on my arm, dragging me across the floor. I woke to stare into the face of a red-eyed wolf.

The demon wolves had found me.

Then I passed out.

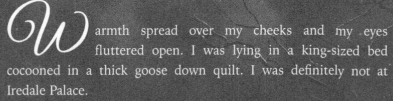

22

*W*armth spread over my cheeks and my eyes fluttered open. I was lying in a king-sized bed cocooned in a thick goose down quilt. I was definitely not at Iredale Palace.

I stared at a thick leather book on a nightstand and realized it was the *Book of Goody*. I went to reach for it.

"So, you're finally awake."

I turned to see a white-haired young woman sitting on a chair. Hades was at her feet, and I was overjoyed to see him. When I saw the red-eyed wolf at her side, though, I scurried across the bed, tangling myself up in the quilt.

The Catalan dragon jumped on the bed, wagging his tail happily.

"Hades?" Was I dreaming? Tears stung my eyes and I wrapped my arms around his neck, hugging him. "You're alive."

"He hasn't left your side for a minute, and as you can see, he kept the *Book of Goody* out of Calvin's hands." She petted the wolf. "This one hasn't left your side, either."

I clung to Hades. "Who are you?"

"I'm Ebony."

If this was Queen Ebony, she didn't look like any queen I had ever met. She was wearing a white tank top, black jeans and high black boots. "The Queen of the Dark Demons?"

She laughed and tilted her head back. "That's one of my titles. But just Ebony will do." She gestured with her hand. "Why did you think Hades was dead?"

I petted his mane. My hand was shaking. "Calvin told me Velkan and the demon wolves murdered my whole team." I glared at the demon wolf sitting at her side. "You shouldn't be by that thing, Hades. No."

The wolf winced, collapsed onto its gut and sighed. I swear it was pouting.

"I think you hurt her feelings." Ebony rubbed the wolf's head and then scratched her ears.

"It's a she?" The wolf looked at me with tears pooling in her eyes.

Ebony nodded. "Yes. This is the demon wolf you healed. You broke the Unseelie spell controlling her." She gave me a teasing smile. "Wow, do you always believe the bad guys so easily?"

"What?" My mind was whirling and I rubbed my sweaty forehead. "I must be dreaming."

Ebony got off her tall leather chair and set at the edge of my bed. She clasped my shaking hand. "No, honey, you're awake. Calvin's an asshole and fucked with your mind, that's all."

I moistened my lips. "So my team..."

"They're not dead. Or at least, not that we know of."

That wasn't reassuring.

"What happened? I remember opening the portal and getting the prisoners out, but nothing more." I squeezed her hand. "Are they all right?"

"Yes, they all made it." She tilted her head. "Look."

I followed her gaze and smiled. Gloria was sound asleep in chair, snoring softly, her head slumped to the side. She still had dark circles under her eyes, but her blonde hair had been washed and her tattered blue dress had been replaced with a white sweater, a red and black plaid skirt and high boots.

"She should be in bed," Ebony said. "But she wanted to be here when you woke. She's stubborn."

Gloria stretched awake and arched her back sleepily. "No more than you are."

I grinned. "Hey, Gloria."

She got up and sat on the other side of my bed. I was surrounded by Ebony, Gunnar, and Gloria and I felt safer than I had in forever.

The red-eyed wolf slowly came over and put her head on my bed.

I looked at her. "So, you saved my ass, huh?"

The wolf wagged her tail. She slipped around Ebony and rested her head on a pillow. I bit my lip, not sure if I should do this, but for some reason, my wolf was pushing at me as if she recognized her. I placed my hand on the wolf's head.

A jolt of energy flashed through me, pumping my blood through me faster and faster. I jerked my head back and shook it hard.

A name echoed in my mind—Luna.

"Salem!" Both Gloria and Ebony cried out.

I passed out again briefly, then woke up to find myself looking into Hades' concerned golden eyes.

I turned my head to see the demon wolf, staring at me with sorrow and whimpering.

I gave her a weak smile. "I know you. You're Luna." Once again, she wagged her tail, thumping it against a night stand.

"We couldn't get her to leave," a male voice said.

I looked up to see a tall man sitting on the same chair that Ebony had been. He had green eyes and short brown hair and had on a three-piece suit. He reminded me of someone, but I couldn't place him.

"I'm sorry, I know I know you, but…"

"I am King Christopher of the Tundra Kingdom—Ashton's father. You're a guest at my home, Highburn Fortress."

I sat taller on the bed. "I'm so sorry."

He looked at me curiously. "For what?"

I lowered my head. "Ashton died protecting me."

"Who told you that? Calvin?" he asked gently.

I lifted my head and hope began to bloom within me. "You mean he's not dead?"

"Not at all. He was badly wounded in the battle at the witch's cabin, but according to Queen Gwendoline, he'll survive."

"She's here, too?"

"Yes, she's been staying at Highburn since the demon wolf pulled you out of the dungeon."

I scratched the demon wolf's ear. "Her name is Luna." A rustle of power slid between us, but this time, it didn't throw me for a loop.

"I heard you say that when you woke up." He motioned with his hand. "She communicated with you?"

"Yes, but she knocked me on my ass first."

He gave me a stern look and I lowered my head. Crap, I remembered now. Ashton's father was a stickler for prim and proper language.

"I'm sorry."

"You're forgiven."

I looked around the dimly-lit room. "Where are Gloria and Ebony?"

"Sleeping. We've taken turns watching over you, but your two faithful companions here have refused to leave you."

I rubbed my eyes. "What time is it?"

"Almost three in the morning."

"I still don't understand all that happened."

"Yes, it's a lot to take in. Gunnar and Ebony were visiting me on a diplomatic mission when Gunnar sensed that Hades was in mortal danger. We came as soon as we could." He sighed and bowed his head. "But not quite soon enough."

"Remi?" My voice croaked.

He held my gaze. "Taken."

I couldn't bring myself to ask about Mateo.

As if reading my mind, he continued. "Mateo and Quint were also captured. So was King Gunnar."

My eyes widened and my head was spinning. "What? Mateo's alive? He's alive?" I put my hand over my chest and burst into tears of relief.

"When we last saw him, yes. But he's been branded a traitor, Salem, and that's not a good thing in the Moon Kingdom."

I took a sobering breath and wiped the tears off my cheeks. "I'm sorry for behaving like a baby."

"Don't be. He's your mate. I don't know how I would feel if someone threatened to kill my mate. I may not always show it, but my queen is my world."

"Do you think...do you think Mateo's already dead?"

God, I don't think I could take it if he said yes.

He was silent for a minute. "I don't know. But I can tell you what I would do if it were me. I would keep him alive and use him as a bait."

"Do you think that's what Calvin's going to do?"

"I'm afraid so. Personally, I wouldn't torture him, but Calvin—"

I gritted my teeth and finished his sentence for him. "Is a monster."

"Yes. And now he's declared war on my kingdom. None of the other kingdoms will support us."

"Are Raven and Lucien here too?"

"Unfortunately, no. They are involved in a mission to retrieve Lucien's brother, Darius, from the Elder Dimension. Otherwise, they would be."

"Are the Dark Demons going to declare war on the Moon Kingdom?"

"They have declared Gunnar a traitor and want to remove him as king, but I suspect Calvin has something to do with this."

This all fucking sucked. "Can they do that?"

"If they have proof of traitorous acts, but it still wouldn't be easy. Gunnar is the rightful heir. I suspect they are hoping to get his sister out of the Hollows and declare her queen."

"You can't be serious?"

"I'm afraid so. The only way to stop this madness is to rescue Gunnar and for you to take your rightful place as queen."

"And my mate, Mateo, would be king."

"Of course. What's your point?"

"He's not royalty. Will you support him as my king consort?"

"There was a time I would not, but times have changed. My eyes have been opened. I will be one of the first kings to support this union, just as I'm the first king to challenge Calvin for his right to the throne. But I need proof. We need the Rose Box. Calvin has it—"

"But he can't open it, and I know where the key is."

Eagerness flared in his eyes. He hurried closer to my bed. "Tell me, Salem. Where is it?"

"Well, I guess it's truer to say I know of someone who knows where the key is."

He frowned. "Who?"

I told him about Hayley's familiar, Freedom.

"I don't recall seeing any bald eagle." He scratched his chin. "Did you?"

"There were birds of prey there," I said. "But I never saw a bald eagle."

"Are you sure the witch was telling the truth?"

"I'm sure of it."

"Curious."

Luna nudged my hand urgently. This was totally weird but I thought she was trying to communicate with me.

"Luna, have you seen a bald eagle at the witch's cabin?"

She licked my hand as if to say yes.

King Christopher and I stared at each other. Neither of us spoke.

Finally, he sighed. "I think you'd better get some rest. We'll talk about this some more in the morning."

I wanted to argue, but my body had other ideas. Weariness crept back into my bones and I slid under the covers with Hades curled up beside me.

I yawned. "Very well."

I drifted off to sleep...

I was walking through the dense forest and I could see the turrets of Iredale Palace. I headed toward the secret entrance at the rear that Mateo had shown me.

Velkan stepped out of the shadows. I gasped.

He had Mateo by the arm. My mate's arms were pinned behind him and he was gagged.

Blood dripped down his mouth and he had ugly welts all over his body, as if he had been whipped repeatedly.

"So, bitch," Velkan growled. "This is your so-called mate. A pathetic, treasonous guard. A traitor."

I lunged. "Leave him alone."

Velkan pulled out a knife and put it to Mateo's throat. "One step closer and he dies."

Three demon wolves stepped in front of Velkan and Mateo, blocking my path.

"You have something that belongs to me. I want her back."

I glared. He was not getting my Luna.

"No."

"Then he dies."

"I've broken the spell. She won't come back to you."
"You have a choice, princess. Your mate or the demon wolf."

I woke up, dripping sweat.

"You were having a nightmare, I think," a female voice said.

Queen Gwendoline sat in the chair, looking as regal as ever. Her white hair was pulled up into a messy bun and she had on a long blue shimmering gown. She stared at me with those sad, gentle eyes that had flicks of stars.

"Where's...where's the king?"

"Asleep. He stayed with you until dawn. Now, it's my turn to keep watch. Tell me about your nightmare."

"It was Velkan...he...he wanted Luna back, or he said he'd kill Mateo."

"Hard choices are upon you, Salem. You are entering the final battle between good and evil."

Luna whined and looked at me pitifully. I had healed her and she had saved my life. How could I give her up again now?

23

The drapes were open and sunlight warmed my face, but not my heart. I sat up in bed, crossed my legs, and reassuringly petted Luna, who was looking terrified. I stared at the queen. "So, you want me to give up Luna?"

Queen Gwendoline smiled. "Did I say that?"

I thought about it. "Well, no..."

"I said hard choices will have to be made, just like they are in every war." Fresh sadness flickered in her eyes and I remembered how she had lost her mate, King Finbar, in the last one. Her son, Rhys, was now king.

"I can't stay in this bed anymore. I can't be lying around here while—" My throat closed up.

She smiled and put her hands out. "Then get up."

I threw back the blankets and prayed I didn't fall on my ass. Luckily, my legs didn't betray me. I looked around the elaborate room, not sure what to do next.

The queen stood. "I assume you would like some fresh clothes and a shower before you leave?"

"Yes, please, but—"

"I have clothes laid out for you in the bathroom."

I turned my head, not sure what else to say. I kept thinking of Mateo and realized even in the nightmare I hadn't been able to tell him I loved him.

Queen Gwendoline came over to me and before I could stop myself, I threw myself in her arms, sobbing. She didn't balk, or walk away. She held me tight as I clung to her, crying softly. I was so sick of the tears but I couldn't stop them. It was as if the sprinklers had been turned on and I couldn't shut them off.

She stroked my hair. "Salem, you're strong. You have the blood of the first king in you." She lifted my chin. "Even if you returned Luna to Velkan, he wouldn't be able to control her anymore. You've bonded with her now, and that's a bond that can't be broken."

I sniffed. "But Velkan bonded with them."

"No, my dear. That was an evil spell, not a bond. Once you break it, all four wolves will be loyal to you and only you. Something that could never happen with Calvin."

"Really?"

"You're the one with the power now. It scares not only Velkan, but Calvin too. Freeing Luna, releasing the prisoners in Calvin's dungeon...neither of those things has ever happened before." She clasped my wet cheeks with her hands. "Do you understand? Never."

"But what about Mateo, Remi, Gunnar, and Quint..."

She kissed my forehead. "You will find a way to victory, Salem. I believe in you. You won't be facing Calvin alone. Remember that."

Mateo flashed in my mind, the way he'd been tortured in my dream. My empty gut churned.

"There's something else, isn't there?"

I clasped my teeth together tight until I was sure I wasn't going to spew bile all over the queen's shimmering blue dress. "I never...I never told Mateo I loved him...and now he could die."

She clasped my chin. "Then you must find him and tell him. You may find that even harder to do then defeating your enemies."

My eyes widened and my chest clenched. Could this woman read my mind?

"You have lived a life without trust, Salem. It's time for you to take a new step in your journey to reclaim your crown." She took my hand and led me to the bathroom. "But for now, wash up, my dear. Your destiny is waiting for you."

I nodded, not sure I wanted to hop in bed with destiny just yet.

The bathroom was just as beautiful as the bedroom, simple and elegant, with a white marble countertop and shower walls and matching white tile floors. Thick gold towels were stacked neatly on the counter.

I smiled when I saw the pile of clothes. Queen Gwendoline knew what I liked—black sweater, a pair of jeans, black lacy bra with matching bikini underwear and tall black cowboy boots. I wasn't into dresses and she didn't make me wear one. I had a feeling that would have been King Christopher's preference, but I wasn't a pampered princess, I was a warrior, ready to fight for my people, my friends, and my mate.

Within seconds, steam filled the bathroom. The hot pulsing shower washed away the filth from Calvin's dungeon. Lavender shampoo and body wash was just what I needed to make me forget the dungeon's stench. I scrubbed my hair and washed myself, inhaling the fragrance, allowing the warm water to ease my tense muscles.

I would have loved to indulge longer in the shower but there would be time enough for that later. My mate needed me and I wasn't going to let him down.

I may have gone into the bathroom broken but I came out a renewed warrior. Queen Gwendoline was gone, but my two besties, Luna and Hades, were waiting for me patiently.

"Are you two ready?"

They both got up immediately and followed me out of the

bedroom. I didn't know where I was, but Hades and Luna seemed to know where they were going, so I let them lead the way and trotted behind them. I inhaled the most delicious smell of eggs, bacon, sausage, and fresh baked bread. My stomach roared with hunger.

Luna and Hades led me into a formal dining room where there were silver chafing dishes on a buffet table. It all smelled delicious, but when I thought of what was happening to Mateo and the others I wasn't sure I could eat a bite.

Ebony and Gloria looked up at me and smiled.

"Good morning." Ebony looked at me over the rim of her coffee cup. Gloria was buttering a croissant. "I was wondering when you'd come down here."

I edged over to the buffet table that had crispy bacon, sausages, scrambled eggs, biscuits with gravy, and fluffy croissants. My stomach roared and my mouth watered, and my wolf whined, wanting to devour everything in sight.

Ebony put her cup down. "I know you're worried, but you have to eat, Salem. The witch's cabin is a long way from here and you don't want to be lagging behind because you didn't eat anything."

I frowned. "You act like you're coming with me."

"Calvin has my mate, Salem. You didn't think I stay behind like a pampered princess, did you?"

"Ashton and I are coming too." Gloria put down her croissant. "My father needs to be stopped."

She still had dark circles under her eyes and her hand holding the croissant twitched.

"Are you sure you're well enough?"

She sighed. "Probably not. But Hayley's still imprisoned and I can't imagine what he's doing. He'll take his anger at losing Luna out on her."

Luna sat next to Gloria and placed her head on her lap.

Gloria petted her. "It's not your fault, Luna. It's my father's. He's a sadistic tyrant that needs to be stopped."

Ebony pointed. "Eat, Salem. Don't force me to tie you up and force feed you."

I put my hands up in surrender. "All right. All right. I'll eat." I got a plate and loaded it up with scrambled eggs, bacon and sausage. My wolf wanted meat and lots of it. I also couldn't resist the biscuits and poured sausage gravy over them. I put my plate on the table. "Where is everyone?" I got a cup of coffee and doctored it with cream.

"King Christopher and Queen Gwendoline are meeting with his advisors," Gloria said. "I think Ashton's there as well."

I frowned as I sat down. "Why weren't we invited?"

"It's the way the wolf kingdom works," Gloria said. "We aren't part of their pack. They are determining how they want to proceed in fighting and protecting their kingdom."

"You mean wolves don't work together?"

"Each pack is different. They are very territorial about their kingdoms, just like wolves in the wild. We protect what's ours," Gloria said. "But when we're collectively threatened, we come together to fight—like during the last Supernatural War with Cormac and the Unseelie."

I finished off two pieces of bacon. "I guess I have a lot to learn about running a kingdom."

"It's not easy," Ebony said sadly. "Especially when you have subjects that don't accept you and perhaps even want to kill you."

"Who is protecting your throne now?" I asked.

"The Freedom Fighters, and my father. He's the Golden Phoenix, and a powerful purple dragon. None of my subjects would dare take him on. But we really have to rescue Gunnar and restore peace. King Calvin has been sending emissaries to round up the Dark Demons and get them to accept his sister as Queen."

I cut into a biscuit dripping with gravy. "Do you think they'll try and break her out of The Hollows?"

"They might try, but they would have to get past the warden Stefan Gabor first. He's a powerful reaper, and Anton and the other Defenders are now involved in protecting The Hollows too, so I think they'll think twice."

"That's good."

"My father's getting desperate, Salem," Gloria said. "Which makes him extremely dangerous. He'll do anything to keep his crown. He'll kill or torture anyone to find the archives."

"Well, he's not going to get into the Rose Box without the key."

Gloria looked at me with tears swimming in her eyes. "Unless he tortures Hayley and she can't hold out any longer."

I cursed under my breath. "Then we have to find Freedom before he does."

Luna thumped her tail excitedly.

I scratched her ear. "Do you know where he is, girl?"

The lines around Ebony's eyes tightened. "If Luna knows, doesn't that mean the other demon wolves do too?"

"They know where a bald eagle is, but they might not know the significance of it."

"Unless Hayley tells him," Gloria pointed out glumly.

Food didn't seem the most important thing on my agenda again.

"Salem, you've barely eaten anything," Ebony said. "You have to eat more."

That suddenly reminded me of Remi and tears swam in my eyes.

"What's wrong?" she asked.

"You reminded me of my aunt just now, is all. It's something she would have said." I put my elbows on the table and rubbed my forehead. "This fucking sucks."

Ebony and Gloria got out of their seats and hugged me. None of us spoke and we just sat there for a while until someone cleared their throat.

Ebony and Gloria released me and we looked up to see King Christopher standing in the doorway, holding a letter in his hand.

His ashen face and the tightness around his lips and mouth didn't bode well. Whatever was in that letter was bad.

I looked up at him. "What's wrong?"

"This just arrived by private messenger."

Gloria sat down and she looked as pale as a ghost. "Is it from my father?"

"Yes, it is." He stretched out his arm. "It's for you, Salem."

I stared at the letter as if it were a coiled snake ready to strike. I pushed myself away from the table and forced myself to stand. Hades and Luna were right at my side. My hand shaking, I took the letter from King Christopher.

M*y dear Salem,*

Y*ou have done me a great injustice by stealing one of my demon wolves, kidnapping my daughter, and freeing prisoners that were enemies of my crown. You have also turned my allies against me, specifically, the Tundra Kingdom.*

These are insults I cannot abide. Therefore, I must teach you a lesson.

Firstly, you will bring the demon wolf with you to Iredale Palace and turn her over to Velkan.

Secondly, you will then face me alone in Iredale Palace's arena. We will fight to the death. If you fail to bring the demon wolf, or bring anyone else, I will execute the prisoners one at a time, starting with your mate, Mateo.

We will meet on the Winter Solstice. Do not disappoint me.

K*ing Calvin*

. . .

I re-read the letter several times. Anger, fear, and sadness churned in my gut, shoving the food up my throat.

"Salem, what does it say?" Ebony demanded.

I swallowed several times before I answered her. I lifted my head. "He's demanded that I return Luna to him and face him alone on the Winter Solstice. If I don't, he'll kill the prisoners, starting with Mateo."

Ebony's face paled. "He'll kill Gunnar next."

"Salem, my father will kill you." Tears slid down Gloria's cheeks. "He's never lost in the Iredale arena. It's where he takes the prisoners that he hates the most. He rips them to pieces in front of his people." Her words were like ice fingers closing around my throat squeezing tighter and tighter, cutting off my air.

Shit, I wasn't going to make it.

I could feel my wolf pushing forward. She had no fear. She wanted to face the king.

King Christopher coughed politely. "I received a letter as well."

The hair on the back of my neck stood up. "You did?"

He nodded. "Calvin's declared war on my kingdom."

I gasped and covered my mouth. "Oh, no. I'm so sorry. This is all my fault."

He shook his head. "No, it's not Salem. He's the one that started this by torturing my son and his would-be mate. That's not something I can tolerate. The die has been cast. We cannot turn back now."

Queen Gwendoline entered the room. I forced myself not to rush into her arms and bawl and shake like a baby. She gave me a gentle smile as if she knew what I was thinking and feeling.

"You all need to have faith. This day has been approaching. The day that Salem would face her uncle and retrieve her crown."

"But my father—"

"Has never lost a match, no," the queen interrupted. "But he also has never faced an opponent that has the power of the first king, either."

I shoved my hand through my hair. "You really think I can beat him?"

"I do." She walked over to Luna and put her palm on her head. "Because the demon wolves will help you."

"I don't understand."

The queen stroked Luna's head. "You must free the other wolves, Salem. They belong to you and you'll be able to draw on their power, like the first king did. Then you will be able to defeat your uncle."

"But I'm drained when I use the *Morphello Refulsi* spell."

"You might not need to use that. I feel the key to victory is in the Rose Box. You must find it before Calvin does."

Chills ran down my spine. "But Calvin has the box."

"Correction," she said. "Velkan has it. And this girl here knows where it is."

Once again, Luna thumped her tail enthusiastically.

I looked at everyone in the room. "But he said I have to face him in the arena alone. If anyone comes with me, he'll kill the prisoners."

Ebony smiled deviously. "There's more than one way to skin a wolf."

"If you try to do this alone, Salem," the queen said, "Calvin wins. He's hoping you'll abandon your friends. It will make it easier for him to kill you and then he'll finish off everyone else."

I lifted my head high and tremors overtook me. My wolf pushed through.

I arched my back and let out a howl.

Aaaaaaooooo

King Christopher and Gloria joined me in my song. Ebony joined us. Hades roared. Ashton rushed into the room in wolf form and joined the howl.

Tingling sensations rushed over me, sending power surged

through me. I realized that it was my team that made me stronger. It's what Calvin feared the most.

The song ended and I looked at everyone. We were bonded. We were stronger together than alone, but we needed to free the others if we wanted to win.

I looked at Gloria with fierce determination. "We're going to free Hayley, too. She's suffered enough and I bet whatever is in that Rose Box will tell us how."

Gloria smiled through her tears and clapped her hands in delight. Ashton rubbed his head against her thigh.

Queen Gwendoline looked around the group. "Well, I think my job here is done. I wish you all success on your journey." She turned to King Christopher. "You won't be fighting in this alone. I will send aid."

"Thank you," he said. "I must prepare for battle." He looked at Ashton. "I give you my blessing to fight with Salem, my son." He bowed slightly. "If you'll excuse me."

He left quickly. I looked at my team. My wolf swelled inside me. She wanted us to lead together. King Calvin had drawn a line, daring me to step over it.

And I would.

At the arena.

On the Winter Solstice.

Prepare to die, asshole

I braced my legs apart and put my hands on my hips. "Let's go find Freedom."

Did you love Wolf Prince? Do you want to see what happens next? Then you'll want to preorder Wolf Mate and see the final conclusion!

Wolf Mate:

My mate is captured and he'll die unless I face my enemy alone.

The final battle is here. I have to prove that I'm worthy of the crown.

Everything rests on me.

But I'm willing to accept the challenge.

I want justice for my parents' murder and my demon wolves' enslavement.

My enemy doesn't play fair, and I know it's an ambush.

Bring it on, dude. Win or lose, I'm ready.

DEAR READER

Thank you for taking a chance on me and reading Salem's story. This is her dark night of the soul where everything goes from bad to worse, but don't worry she and Mateo will get their happily ever after ending.

I really enjoyed bringing everyone back from my other stories like Raven, Lucien, Anton, and Ebony! I will always have a trickle in of the other characters since this is one big universe.

If you never want to miss a new release from me, then sign up for my newsletter and become a Legacy! You'll get the first book in the series that it stared it all—Legacy Academy: The Early Years!!

I also have a private Facebook if you would like to come and play with me. I have giveaways and we just have fun. This is another way for you to become a Legacy!

I hope I'll see you around!

M Guida

ABOUT THE AUTHOR

M Guida has always loved fantasy and romance, especially dragons. Growing up, she devoured fantasy books and all kinds of young adult books. And then she found romance and a whole new world opened up to her.

Now as an adult, she fell in love with academy romance and has blended all of her past loves into one compelling series. Dragons, vampires, elves, demons, and shifters all attend Legacy Academy.

When she's not writing, she lives in the colorful Rocky Mountains with her fur baby, Raven, and enjoys taking her for walks.

If you never want to miss a new release, sign up for her newsletter and get Legacy Academy The Early Years for free!

ALSO BY M GUIDA

Wolf Princess:

Wolf Princess

Wolf Prince

Wolf Mate

Academy for Reapers:

Academy for Reapers Year One

Academy for Reapers Year Two

Academy for Reapers Year Three

Academy for Reapers Year Four

Legacy Series:

Before Legacy: The Early Years

Legacy Year One

Legacy Year Two

Legacy Year Three

Legacy Year Four

Ebony's Legacy Year One

Ebony's Legacy Year Two

Ebony's Legacy Year Three

Ebony's Legacy Year Four

Collections:

Legacy Academy Collection One

Before Legacy Series:

Before Legacy: Armond

Before Legacy: Gunnar

The Defenders

Wolf Defender

Vella Story:

Bite Me: Vampire's Forbidden Romance